MISTLETOE WALTZ

A WALTZ WITH DESTINY: BOOK THREE

ALANNA LUCAS

ISBN 978-1-956367-06-5

Sebastiani Press

PO Box 1234

Simi Valley, Ca 93062

Cover by Dar Albert

❀ Created with Vellum

For Josie

CHAPTER 1

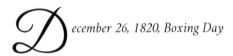 *ecember 26, 1820, Boxing Day*

"THANK YOU, my lady. Primrose is my favorite color!" Faith's lady's maid exclaimed with a combination of surprise and joy. "I've never had fabric this lovely before." The tears in Troth's eyes spoke volumes, and it warmed Faith's heart to see the effect her gifts had. Everyone at Deer Park had been so welcoming since her arrival four months ago. Not having had a lady in residence for twenty-five years, they were eager to please, and Faith wanted to show her appreciation for all they had done.

"And this is for you, Caspar. Thank you for your dedicated service." The look of disbelief when he opened his gift filled Faith with delight. Although this was a foreign world to her, it was just how she had imagined Boxing Day would be at all the grand estates. It had been such a joyous day for her and she could not keep the smile off her face.

"Lady Hawthorne, I don't know what to say." Caspar ran his hand across the small, dark brown leather book.

"You're most welcome, Caspar." As she turned to pick up another gift from the adorned table, her skirt brushed Balder's head. The dog looked up at her but did not raise his head from the ornate jonquil rug, his black wirehair coat a bold and direct contrast to the rug's vibrant colors.

Just then, a cool breeze whipped through the room, sending a shiver down her spine.

Pine and leather invaded her senses. Even before she turned toward the source, she knew her husband had returned to Deer Park.

Balder jumped to a sitting position, his ears perked up, a slight snarl rumbling past his jaws. Faith patted his head as much for his comfort as for hers.

A moment later, she heard the deep masculine voice of her husband growling at her. "What are you doing?"

Swallowing hard, she turned to face him. He stood larger and more handsome than she remembered, but his honey-colored eyes were not as soft and caring as they had been on the first night when she'd met him. She feared that gentleness and compassion had gone forever.

Her pulse increased, and her stomach lurched. Her first instinct was to run. She detested confrontations, they always ended the same way. Fighting back tears, she continued to stroke Balder's head, and desperately tried to maintain her composure in front of the servants.

"Happy Christmas, my lord." Her voice cracked with each word. Waving her hand toward the presents, she explained, "I was just handing out gifts to the staff."

"I can see that." Lord Hawthorne's tone was stern, harsh… cold. His eyes bore into her. The longer he stared at her, the more uncomfortable she felt. And then he strolled up to her, his tall form towering over her petite figure.

She wanted to run and hide. It was her fault that he was unhappy. It was her carelessness that had got them both into this situation.

The seconds ticked by. Faith hoped the floor would open up and swallow her whole. Perhaps then she would find some peace.

"Finish, and then I would like a word with you in my study."

All speech escaped her. She nodded in acquiescence and then turned to continue handing out the gifts. Dread sank further into the pit of her stomach, and her shoulders slumped in defeat. She had decorated Deer Park, hoping that her husband would spend Christmas at the house *and* be pleased with her efforts. Out of the corner of her eye, she watched him storm off. She took in a deep, jagged breath. *It will be alright.*

No one said a word now that the lively festive atmosphere had dissipated. All that remained was a dull silence, interrupted only by the sound of footsteps as servants came forth to receive their boxes.

By the time Faith presented the last gift, all efforts to maintain composure had failed. Her knees were wobbling and she could not contain the tremors that crept up her body. She detested the look of pity she saw in all their eyes. She did not want their sympathy, she wanted respect. But most of all, she wanted acceptance and love.

Troth cast a consoling look at her. Over the past months, the woman had become more than just a lady's maid, she'd become a trusted friend. She was the only person in the world who knew Faith's secret.

Sucking in a deep breath, Faith could no longer delay the inevitable. The time had come to face her husband.

A slow funeral march played over and over in her head as she walked toward her imminent doom. The walls inched closer about her with each step she took, and the fragrant evergreen air stifled her breathing. "It will be fine. He will not be like Father," she murmured to herself. Except for his temper, Lord Hawthorne had never given her cause to fear him. *Just like Father before Mary died.*

Shaking that thought from her mind, she smoothed the front of her dress with unsteady hands. Turning the corner, she gazed down the long, dark hall.

Weighed down with fear, she had to convince her legs to move forward. "It will be fine," she chanted softly to herself over and over.

She stopped and, standing frozen in place, stared at the dark mahogany door, debating her next course of action. For one brief moment, she thought to run in the opposite direction and find a safe hiding spot.

With one hand resting on the elegant brass knob, she tried to convince herself once again. *I can do this.* She closed her eyes, attempting to numb the feelings that were lashing through her body. "He is not Father," she murmured to herself. *He is not like Father.*

MARCUS, the Marquess of Hawthorne, paced the length of the room for the umpteenth time. How dare she give gifts to *his* servants without his permission? Then his conscience reminded him they were now her servants too, but that was a whole other matter. He shook his head. And his dog had actually growled at him. The traitor had growled at *him*!

Running a hand through his hair, he scolded himself. *What the hell am I doing here?* He detested the effect his wife had on him. He had spent years avoiding such emotions, and in one evening, all his efforts had been thrown out of the carriage and trampled upon by a dozen horses.

After his hasty marriage four months ago, he'd hied his

unwanted bride off to the country and returned to London, hoping his family would not discover what he had done. It had been two months since his last disastrous visit to Deer Park. He had tried to stay away, but for the life of him, he could not. He didn't want to *want* to see her. His unwanted wife may have been out of sight these past couple of months, but she was never far from his thoughts. How could she be?

The night they'd first met in London still haunted him. He had never been so attracted to a woman in his entire life. She had been wearing the same pale blue gown she wore tonight. He had barely been able to keep his wits about him then, and the effect had only worsened this evening. The blue gown deepened the color of her eyes, and her fair blonde hair shimmered like freshly fallen snow on a moonlight night. From the start, her sweet nature and bashful glances had mesmerized him.

It was all a lie, his heart chided. He should have known better. *Her father tricked you into marrying her,* he reminded himself. Every instinct told him she was just a victim, but his heart convinced him she could not be trusted.

Where is she? His patience was hanging by a thread.

He eyed the stack of responsibilities piled on his desk. He should not have neglected his duties for so long. Sifting through the correspondences, he tossed the ones that did not need his immediate attention aside, next to the small holly and ivy centerpiece. "What is keeping her?" he grumbled to himself. Patience was not one of his attributes.

Throwing the rest of the envelopes down, he marched to the door, grabbed the knob, and pulled the door open wide. A petite figure tumbled forward into his arms. The world stood still for a moment as vanilla enraptured his senses. His hands ached to explore, to claim what was his.

She pulled away with haste. A red blush stained her cheeks. "I apologize. I..."

"What took you so long?" The words came out more harshly than he intended. He turned his back on her, not wanting her to see that she had discomposed him, and strolled to his desk.

"I…I was handing out the gifts, and..." Her voice quavered, then died away.

Marcus took his seat and sucked in a deep breath. He needed to gain control of his emotions. "Who gave you the liberty to decorate *my* house, present gifts to *my* staff, and God knows what else?" His voice reverberated through the room and, with each word that bellowed from his mouth, his wife took a small step back.

What was she hiding? He was convinced something nefarious was going on in his home, behind his back.

"It is Christmastide and…" Her words trailed off and she began to worry her bottom lip.

He would not fall for that ploy. He would not succumb to any of her enticements. Narrowing his gaze on her, he waited for her to finish speaking.

The silence dragged out for several seconds before she continued. "I thought it would be a pleasant surprise." Her eyes were wet with unshed tears.

Don't fall for this charade. A woman's tears would not fool him again. Not ever again.

Her gaze shifted downward, and she stared at the rug, clasping the sides of her dress. When she finally looked up and spoke, her voice was soft and meek, almost unsure. "I…I was hoping you would be pleased and… I just wanted to celebrate Christmastide, my lord."

His temper reached a new height the moment she began to weep. How dare she come into his house and stir memories he'd buried deep into the recesses of his mind. She had even decorated his study!

His fists tightened. He wanted to hit something. Slamming his hand down on the desk with more force than he intended, he stood and walked around the desk. His wife flinched and closed her eyes. That behavior took him aback.

Lady Hawthorne, his wife only in name, stood with her eyes shut tight, a grimace encompassing her features. She was trembling from head to toe, swaying from side to side. Something was not quite right. Concern nibbled at his conscience.

Standing in front of her, he softened his tone. "Open your eyes." With her head still hung low, she did as he commanded. A stream of tears continued anew. She flinched again as he tucked his index finger under her chin.

When he raised her chin, she stared at him with questioning, almost terrified, eyes. He did not know what he was looking for, so he squinted and leaned in closer. Her scent was sweet and enticing, and her skin glowed against the soft candlelight.

Pulling away, she cried, "Please don't!" Before he could say a word, she ran to the door, flung it open, and scurried into the darkness.

Go after her.

His damn conscience should mind its own business!

Guilt pressed against his chest. Perhaps he had been too harsh. Running a frustrated hand through his hair, he walked with reluctance toward the door. Best to deal with this now.

He had only taken a couple of steps when Caspar entered, silver tray in hand. "This has just arrived for you, my lord. The young man said it was urgent and is waiting for an answer."

What, now? He had not even been home for half a day, and he was being bombarded with problems. He took the missive from the salver and tore it open. Pinching the bridge of his nose, he took in a deep breath.

Damn his cousin.

"Send him in."

AN HOUR LATER, after one scandal was averted, it was now time to deal with his wife. He didn't know what he was going to say yet, but he would do his best not to lose his temper… again. This place brought back too many childhood memories that he'd rather forget. He shook those distant thoughts away and summoned Caspar to the study.

"Fetch Lady Hawthorne. Tell her I wish to speak with her immediately."

Caspar did not question or look twice as he set about his task, while Marcus began to formulate in his head what he was going to say. Time and again, Faith had declared that she'd had no knowledge of her father's actions. Regardless, he needed to extract the truth before his aunt or grandmother discovered what he had done.

Twenty minutes ticked by and his mood did not improve. Lady Hawthorne was keeping him waiting for the second time in one evening. His rehearsed speech sounding, in his own mind, more like an interrogation than the conversation he was hoping to have.

At the sound of Caspar clearing his throat, he turned around. "She is nowhere to be found."

"It is ten o'clock at night. What do you mean, she is nowhere to be found?" The words rumbled past his lips.

"Troth said Lady Hawthorne returned to her room over an hour ago, visibly upset. She asked to be left alone." Caspar held out a scribbled note. "Troth found this on the bed."

Marcus grabbed the letter from Caspar. The two words jumped off the page and punched him in the gut.

I'm sorry.

Why would she apologize and then leave? Those two

words echoed in his head. Had he really been that cruel to her? The events of the evening, the one-sided argument, and his reaction to her thoughtfulness toward the servants all spun through his mind, confusing his already muddled thoughts. *I'm sorry.* He had heard those words before from another woman who'd broken his heart over twenty years ago. He didn't know what to believe.

He walked to the window. The full moon illuminated the slumbering landscape and the coldness of winter emanated through the glass. Dark clouds had begun to roll in, consuming the night stars. She wouldn't dare venture out on a night like this, would she?

One thing was for certain, he could not live with himself if something should happen to her. Despite the way everything had happened between them, he was still responsible for her.

And you care for her.

He shook that thought away. "Gather the men together. I want her found tonight."

CHAPTER 2

A frigid wind whipped through the countryside, signaling a storm was approaching. Faith hoisted herself onto Frigga, questioning her sanity for leaving so abruptly. After ensuring the pouch that held her meager funds was tightened at her waist, she pulled her cloak closer to her chest and began her flight into the unknown.

"What… choice do I… have?" she questioned herself through chattering teeth, the winter cold already seeping through her body. "I can't stay. I can't…"

The moment Lord Hawthorne's hand had struck the desk, thoughts of her father slamming his hand down on the dining table moments before he'd reached across and grabbed her had ricocheted through her mind.

I won't stay.

Faith knew all too well the pain of staying. She could not face that again. These past months had opened her eyes to a different kind of life, one in which fear did not dictate her every movement. She did not want to see her father ever again, had been avoiding his letters. Since moving to Deer Park, she'd discovered an inner strength that she did not know she had. A year ago, she would have never contemplated leaving any environment.

Although Lord Hawthorne had never directly threatened or raised a hand to her, she could not escape the fear that he would become just like her father. Worse still, that same tingling she'd felt the first night she met him at the theatre had intensified each time he was near.

Why did he have to affect her so? Too many different emotions toiled within—he was handsome with eyes like honey and the staff had all praised his generosity, but his temper caused her despair. Troth had told her to have patience, that Lord Hawthorne would come around, that he was a good man who would never cause her harm.

The full moon lit her way as the sounds of night closed in about her. A deep shiver reached into her very core. She *must* be insane. Why else would she run away in the dead of winter? She could not remember ever being this cold in her entire life.

Frigga carried on at an even canter, seemingly oblivious to the temperature. Faith wanted to put as much distance between herself and Lord Hawthorne, *and* her father, as possible. She determined she would ride to the coast and book passage to…

"I d…don't know where. Any… where b…but here," she rattled out to herself. "P…perhaps some p…place war…rm."

Under normal circumstances—and warmer weather—she would have found much solace in talking to herself. She clenched her teeth together, but that only seemed to cause her body to shiver more.

The moist damp air had seeped into her clothing. Dark clouds rolled across the sky, extinguishing the moonlight. Her entire being filled with dread. She prayed she would survive this night. A flash of lightning in the far distance caught her attention, and a painful image fought its way to the forefront of her mind. She'd tried so hard to block out those recollections and that pain. But on stormy nights like this, it all came back, every unpleasant memory.

Heavy raindrops fell from the angry sky, saturating her clothes. Her prayers were to go unanswered. Another bolt of lightning illuminated the horizon and thunder rolled in furious protest, striking fear in her heart. Frigga reared in agitation and panic at the commotion.

"Easy, girl." Faith rubbed the horse's neck while speaking the calming words. Another streak of lightning flashed, followed by a loud crack. The horse threw her head back.

Faith struggled to keep her seat, her heart pounding wildly in her chest. She tightened her grip on the reins, hoping she could hold on. Frigga was stamping her feet, snorting, and neighing fiercely. Then the horse reared again in terror. "Shh…" Before Faith could get the comforting words out, Frigga bucked, sending her flying forward.

Her body hit the hard ground. As she leaned her head against her sore and aching arms, the sounds of Frigga galloping away echoed in her mind, but she had not the strength or will to get up.

"MY LORD, MY LORD!" A panicked echo resonated from the front of the house.

Perhaps his wife had been found and the search could be called off, but something in his gut told him otherwise. Marcus looked up at the ceiling and closed his eyes. *Please let her be safe.*

"My lord!" He opened his eyes and hurried in the direction of the shouts, almost colliding with Thomas.

"Lady Hawthorne's horse has returned," the young man labored out, his face grave.

Dread sank into the pit of Marcus' stomach. "And Lady Hawthorne?"

Breathing heavily, Thomas shook his head.

Marcus did not wait a moment longer. He may not have wanted this marriage, but she was still his responsibility. "What direction did the horse come from?"

"South, my lord."

Running to the stables, with Thomas following close behind, he reissued his orders. "I'll go south. Tell the others to spread out in all directions. No one is to rest until she is found."

His horse was already being saddled. Not wanting to delay his departure, he pushed the stable boy aside and took over, finishing the task himself. The weather had taken a turn for the worse and there was no time to lose.

Almost an hour had passed and Marcus still had not found her. He had covered quite a distance. Although the rain was coming down in icy sheets, his horse sloshed through the mud at a quick and steady pace. He spotted a dilapidated barn in the distance and hoped his wife had sought shelter from the storm there. It took several minutes for him to reach the ragged old half-standing structure.

There was no sign of life. *Damn.*

He did not linger, but furthered his search. How far could she have gone on such a dreary night?

The heavy rain gave way to an eerie fog that crept over the land. A movement on the ground in the distance caught his attention. He squinted into the hazy mist and his breath caught in his throat, his breathing almost stopping altogether. "Bloody hell." He kicked his horse into a gallop.

Seconds later, he reached the heap on the road. He jumped off his horse and rushed to his wife's side. She was cold and wet, but still breathing. Relief washed through him. *She was alive.* Taking off his coat, he wrapped her in its warmth. Her eyes fluttered open. Instead of the expected relief, he saw a flash of terror before she tried to push herself away from him.

Puzzlement lanced through him. For the second time in one evening, she had pulled away from him in fear.

"D…don't h…hu…rt m…" Her words trailed off into a hoarse whisper. Her face was ashen, eyes still bright with fright. That look struck a chord with him.

He sat back on his haunches and stared at her, shaking his head with disbelief. Did she really believe he would search for her only to cause her harm? Not for the first time did he wonder what she was hiding. He was the one who'd sacrificed his own happiness so that she would not be ruined. He was the one who'd saved her—twice now.

A shiver rippled through her, forcing his attention to the present. Now was not the time or place to uncover those secrets. He needed to get her back to the house. The moment he ran his hands up her legs, her eyes opened wide. Ignoring her shock, he continued with his brief inspection of her body. Satisfied with the results, he informed her, "It doesn't appear that you have broken anything."

She did not respond to him with words, just nodded her head in agreement. He picked up her tiny, shivering frame. Remorse gnawed at his conscience as anger and confusion collided within, conflicting with reason. *What have I done?*

He placed her atop his horse, Ameriko, and then mounted behind her. She tensed the moment their bodies touched and tried to edge away. "I…I can w…walk," she stammered out.

Ignoring her protest, he brought her in close, wrapping his coat more securely about her form. He did not know what had possessed her to leave, but was certain it had something to do with their argument. Why else would the chit have left the warmth of Deer Park? Yes, he was upset over the decorations, but deep down, he knew it had nothing to do with them.

He did not like the emotions this unwanted wife stirred in him. He had buried those feelings for a reason, and every time he was near her, she chiseled away another fine layer. This would have to stop. He might be married to her, but he did not have to offer any affection.

I will not care.

They had only traveled a short distance when a new torrent of rain cascaded down on them. Faith shuddered against him. He felt rather than heard her teeth chatter from the cold.

Damn, this was not good.

The wind pushed them back. Ameriko was a strong horse, but he was showing signs of exhaustion, and they still had a good distance to cover. Marcus determined it would be best if they waited out the worst of the storm. He guided his horse toward the dilapidated structure he had searched earlier.

By the time they reached the crumbling barn, his wife was shaking uncontrollably.

He did not have any means to build a fire, not to mention that everything around them had been drenched to the point of complete saturation. After tending to Ameriko, he pulled a small wool blanket from the saddlebag.

"Take off the coats."

If she was taken aback by his request, she hid it well. Casting her eyes downward, she removed his coat and extended it to him. The silence grew around them as she peeled off her own sodden coat. Her movements were slow, hesitant; first one arm, then the other. Her actions entranced Marcus. Taking in deep, steady breaths, he tried to focus on their situation and not on her.

Once she was divested of her coat, Marcus wrapped the blanket about her. "Why don't you get some rest?"

She walked over to a dry spot and curled up on the ground, never taking her eyes off him.

Marcus could not turn away from her questioning gaze. She was such a conundrum to him. He did not know what to think. He did not know her, and before this moment, had almost convinced himself that he really did not care to get to know her.

The silence between them lingered painfully on. It was clear Faith had no intention of speaking to him, but at least she was not cowering in the corner as she had done earlier in the evening.

More than an hour passed before the rain stopped and the fog began to lift. Wanting to get his wife back to the house with all due haste, Marcus went to her, picked her up, and carried her to Ameriko. Thankfully, she did not make a fuss or pull away.

Before too long, the lights of Deer Park could be seen blazing in the distance. It would appear that the entire household was still awake, awaiting Lady Hawthorne's safe return.

"We're almost there." He felt her body heave with a sigh of relief. However, remorse continued to gnaw at him. "I apologize for losing my temper earlier."

Turning her head, she did not say a word, but gave him a simple smile of forgiveness, and then nuzzled her head against his shoulder. That smile touched his heart more than he was willing to admit. What was he going to do?

CHAPTER 3

$\mathcal{T}$he Stone Hall was the last place that Marcus would have thought to look for his wife. Reserved for banquets, it had not been used since before he was born. When he entered the vast space, he was taken aback at its transformation. The pristine white marble walls, sculpted over-mantel, and elegant stucco ceiling faded against the brilliant greenery, and intertwined holly and ivy sprayed throughout. The hall—once cold from disuse—had come alive with the scent of fresh evergreens and hints of clove. It was like a scene from his early childhood, before things had changed.

In front of the large white marble fireplace with the glowing Yule Log sat his wife, absorbed in her own thoughts. Stroking Balder's head, she was gazing upward at the dancing putti detailed in the stuccowork. A pang of jealousy ripped through him. He wanted to know her inner thoughts.

He cleared his throat. "You appear recovered from last night." She didn't, not really. She looked dazed and out-of-sorts, but he did not know what else to say.

Countless seconds passed before she responded, "Yes, my

lord." She lowered her head, cheeks reddened. "I… I'm sorry to have caused so much trouble."

He stepped in closer. Balder raised his head and eyed him, almost as if warning him. Inwardly, he shook his head at the dog. *Traitor.*

"Why did you run away?" The words left his mouth before he could stop them. He hadn't meant to sound like he was interrogating her.

Her cheeks deepened a shade, and she glanced away. Her chest rose and fell as her breathing increased. "I know how unhappy you are with me, and I thought…" She shook her head as she softly continued, "…if I weren't here to make you angry then perhaps you could find happiness…" Her words trailed off to an inaudible murmur.

A dagger of guilt and shame pierced his conscience. He had no idea how to respond to her without giving something of himself away. He desperately wanted to trust her, to believe that she was the sweet young woman who'd entranced him all those months ago, but his heart warned him against it. He sucked in a deep breath and sat next to her.

She edged a couple of inches away, closer to Balder.

Why did she fear him?

"*You* didn't make me angry, you just reminded me of—" He clamped his jaw tight, not wanting to relive the past.

"When your parents were alive."

His mouth fell open. Those words were the last he'd ever expected to hear, but were closer to the truth than he cared to admit. *How did she know?* His bewilderment must have shown.

"Mrs. Gardner, a widow from the local village, told me you were just a boy when they died."

The sorrow and empathy he saw in her eyes touched a part of him he thought had withered. But he still did not want to talk about his life—past or present.

Changing the subject, he waved a hand and inquired, "Why did you do all this?"

His wife glanced about the room, her brilliant smile warming the cool marble space. "This is my favorite time of year. After my mama died, my sister tried to bring happiness back into the house." She shrugged one shoulder as she continued to explain. "She always said that Christmas was a magical time. All year we looked forward to decorating the house on Christmas Eve and bringing in the Yule Log. I thought *if* you returned to Deer Park, you might like…" She worried her lip before continuing, "Well, Mrs. Gardner had commented on how lovely the house looked when your mother was alive."

Who was this mystery widow who seemed to know a great deal about his family? He opened his mouth, the question of who Mrs. Gardner was lingering on his tongue, but then he thought better of it. This was the most conversation they'd ever had, and he didn't want to spoil the moment. He would have Caspar investigate the widow.

"Where does your sister live? Would you care to invite her?"

She stood abruptly and walked over to the fireplace. With her back turned to Marcus, she sighed. "She's dead, my lord." The sadness in her voice wrenched his heart.

As much as he hated to admit it, he felt a certain obligation toward her, and with each passing minute he spent in his wife's company, that feeling grew. Perhaps he wasn't the ogre he thought himself to be.

Taking in a deep breath, pushing his own anxieties further into the recess of his soul, he went to where she stood at the fireplace. In that moment, he wanted nothing more than to hold her, to ease her pain. In the end he settled for, "I did not mean to upset you."

She shook her head and sniffled. "I miss her. I miss Mary

so much." She continued to adjust an already perfect garland, her movements so reminiscent of his late mother's.

She was stirring too many unwanted emotions in him from the past. This was why he rarely came to Deer Park. It was also the reason why he'd chosen to deposit her here after their hasty wedding. Out of sight, out of mind. He knew with certainty that although he had just arrived, he could not stay. He would leave her to enjoy the season with his traitorous dog.

He might regret this decision later, but since he would not be here, he offered a peace offering. She might as well have the pleasure of the season. "I want you to finish decorating the house for Twelfth Night."

She swiveled her head and met his gaze. The joy in her eyes grew with each breath she took. "Oh…" Her words stopped short. Clasping her hands together, she glanced about and then itemized all the things that still needed to be accomplished. "I should get more ribbon for the garlands and, of course, more greenery for…" She started to walk away, and then turned back to him, her smile warming the darkest corners of his soul. "Thank you, Lord Hawthorne."

He was at a loss over his wife. She'd offered no substantial explanation for running away last night, but then had rewarded him with a brilliant smile. And then there was that scene just now, which had only added to his confusion. Although he was determined not to fall under her spell, she continued to plague his every thought.

Making his way to his study, he hoped to address the most urgent of the waiting correspondences before he departed that afternoon. He opened the door. A sudden coldness struck him. The hair on the back of his neck stood on ends with the unforeseen arrival of his aunt.

"Happy Christmas, Aunt Lou. What an unexpected…" *Unwanted surprise.*

"Save the pleasantries, Marcus," Aunt Lou commanded.

Marcus had avoided his aunt on Christmas Eve, managing to sneak away from London in the wee hours, but it would seem he was now about to pay for those actions.

"Why are you avoiding your obligations?" Aunt Lou stood, shoulders back, chin held high. She was braced, as if waiting for an argument to begin.

He would not give her the satisfaction. "I am not avoiding anything, Aunt Lou. I have just had a lot of pertinent business." He sensed his aunt did not believe his excuse.

"Glad to hear that, my boy." She smoothed an errant strand of white hair while continuing to speak. "The decorations look lovely. Troth has done a wonderful job. She has always had a knack for such things."

It wasn't Troth. It was my wife, the woman I've managed to keep secret from you these past months. The situation was beginning to spiral downward, and he didn't know how to regain control before it got worse.

"I've brought mistletoe from Knollwood. The guests will be arriving shortly, and…"

"Guests?" Marcus hoped he'd misheard. But then it dawned on him that his aunt had no intention of leaving and would be in residence for the whole of the yuletide, along with his wife. This was going to be quite the challenge.

"When I learned you were not coming to Knollwood, I invited Arte and Nigel to join us here."

His head began to ache. He raised a brow at her audacity.

"I needed reinforcements to ensure that you see to your obligations, and not run off again. Nigel is the only man I know who could persuade you." Nigel was Marcus' best friend and the husband of his favorite cousin. "They will arrive tomorrow from Kettleworth and break their journey here before we *all* continue on to Knollwood, where everyone else will join us for the festivities until Twelfth Night."

He adored his aunt, but she had overstepped her boundaries. "Why the sudden interest in my life, Aunt Lou?"

"Your grandmother wants you married. You cannot avoid your duties any longer. Either you deal with me or her." Aunt Lou walked up to him and tapped his cheek. "I think I am a better choice."

The thumping in his head increased with each breath he took. How was he to explain the fact he had a wife? Rubbing the back of his neck with his hand, Marcus began, "There is something you should know." His aunt stared at him, waiting for the next sentence, as he inhaled, searching his mind for something—anything—to say that would not make the situation worse.

I'm already married, echoed in the deep crevices of his mind and before he could stop them, the words flowed freely from his mouth.

"I'm married."

For the first time that Marcus could ever recall, his aunt was speechless. Alarms were echoing in his head. He braced himself for screams and arguments, but none were forthcoming.

Several silent seconds passed before he spoke up again. "Perhaps I should explain."

"That would be helpful." He heard the hurt tone in her voice, and it pained him to know that he caused her grief. She had always been there for him, loved him.

He could not very well tell her the truth. She would be livid. Some variation should be acceptable. "Miss Whitworth and I met in London at the theatre. We were introduced by Lady Jefferson."

The questioning look on his aunt's face spoke volumes: *Why would you want to move in the same social circle as that scandal-ridden gossipmonger?* That was an even longer story. *Stay with the facts,* he reminded himself.

"We happened across each other at a coaching inn a couple of days later." That *was* true. Perhaps weaving a convincing tale would not be too difficult after all. "It was love at first sight." That *was* a stretch. He *had* been instantly attracted to Faith, but love at first sight? Marcus did not know if he was even capable of such a thing as love.

Aunt Lou's eyes narrowed as she raised a questioning brow at him.

Revert back to the truth.

"Miss Whitworth—my wife—has a kind heart." It was the absolute truth. He'd received weekly updates from his steward on how she was faring at Deer Park, how she'd brought joy to those around her, and how much the staff adored her. And although he was upset with her for handing out the Boxing Day gifts, she had taken the initiative, even decorating the house for the festive season. He couldn't fault her for that.

Aunt Lou's features relaxed.

Marcus continued on, "After our brief meeting, I knew…" *I could save her.* The thought hit him like a brick to the face. Although Faith appeared content at Deer Park, there was an underlying sadness in her that tore at his heart. "I knew she was the one."

Aunt Lou flashed him a disbelieving smile. "I look forward to meeting your bride this evening."

Marcus watched his aunt stroll out of the room, clearly pleased with herself. He could not believe that she'd accepted his explanations without so much as an argument. For once, Fate was on his side. Now all he had to do was convince Lady Hawthorne to play the part of a doting wife.

After ringing for Caspar, he took the opportunity to contrive a plausible plan to persuade Faith to participate in the farce. It would be to her benefit as well. Winning over his aunt would allow her the freedom to continue on as mistress of the house long after he'd taken his leave. If Aunt Lou suspected their marriage to be a masquerade, then she would do everything in her power to change that, and Marcus did not believe he was up for that challenge.

First things first. He needed to solve the mystery of the widow, then he would speak with his wife.

"Pardon, my lord, you wanted to see me?" his proficient butler questioned as he entered the room.

"Yes. I was wondering if you happen to know of a widow, a Mrs. Gardner, whom Lady Hawthorne met?"

Caspar's features stilled. He cleared his throat and, in a composed manner, answered, "No, my lord."

Marcus could not ascertain why, but he doubted Caspar's response. What could the butler be hiding? Crossing his arms, he took two steps closer to Caspar. Much to Casper's credit, he did not back away or waver.

"Discover who she is."

"Yes, my lord." Caspar stared straight ahead, his features firm and in control, revealing nothing.

Marcus did not have the luxury of time to probe deeper into this matter of the widow himself. He would wait for Caspar's report. He had bigger worries at the moment, namely his wife and aunt.

"Where is Lady Hawthorne?" He had not seen her since their encounter that morning.

Glancing at the clock on the mantel, Caspar informed him, "Lady Hawthorne should still be in the orangery."

He swallowed hard. "The orangery?" It was common knowledge throughout his household just how much he detested that place. Images of a young boy sneaking in and crying himself to sleep plagued his mind.

"Yes, my lord. Lady Hawthorne usually spends most of the day there. Shall I have Thomas fetch her?"

As much as Marcus would have liked that, he needed to speak to his wife *before* his aunt found her. The orangery, at the very least, provided the necessary privacy to talk. Resigning himself to the unfortunate task, he responded, "No, I will go to her myself."

He would have found the look of utter shock on Caspar's normally stoic features quite amusing if it was in regard to anything else.

CHAPTER 4

*S*mall pools of water dotted the path, further evidence of the severity of last night's storm. The ground crunched beneath Marcus' heavy footfall, his chest tightening with each step he took. He had not ventured this way in years—twenty-five years, to be exact.

Glaring at the orangery's ornate metal and glass door, he reached for the handle, but pulled back his hand with a grunt, and then turned around. He paced back and forth several times, breathing in the cool winter air. He was in a foul mood. He did not want to be here. Every chirp, every rustle, every sound from nature was magnified.

His head throbbed, and his insides gurgled. *You're a grown man. The past cannot hurt you.*

Grabbing for the handle once again, Marcus sucked in his breath and entered. Warm, earthy air welcomed him into the vast space.

No sounds of his mother haunting him from the dead disturbed him. The place was peaceful, calm. He stood for several minutes regaining his composure and his heart slowed to a steady, even pace. *Mother is not here*. He released the breath he did not know he was holding.

Glancing about, he saw new life thriving all around him. He had assumed, rather incorrectly, it would seem, that the interior would be in ruins.

Exotic plants lined the perimeter. Rose bushes in a dozen varieties filled the center rectangle. The pathways were swept clean. Even some of the palms he remembered from his childhood were still there and prospering.

Off to one side was his favorite spot where he sat and watched his mother when he was a lad. She often brought huge soft pillows for him to rest on while she'd tended her plants for hours at a time. Shaking off those bittersweet memories, he ventured farther along. He heard his wife's faint voice in the distance beyond the grapevines.

"If we move this one here…" There was a long pause before he heard her grunt and then continue with her sentence. "Perfect. Now, I think that one should…"

Following the sound of her voice, careful not to be seen, he slunk across a couple of interlocking pathways near to where his wife was standing. He had been certain she was hiding something or someone, and now he would have his answer. Why else would she be here, except for the same purpose for which his mother had used this orangery?

Concealed behind a trellis of black grapes, he stretched his neck, trying to see whom she was talking to, but he could not see anyone else present.

Before he had a chance to get closer, his wife whipped around, letting out a cry. "Oh, my lord, you startled me." She clutched her hand to her bosom, which rose and fell with heavy breathing. Something stirred within him and improper images flooded his mind. *Damn these thoughts.*

He began in what he hoped was an innocent tone, "I beg

your pardon. I didn't mean to startle you. Who were you talking to just now?"

She glanced about in confusion. The space between her brows crinkled in a most endearing way. Her cheeks reddened, and lowering her head, she glanced at the floor before looking up at him with sparkling blue eyes. "I was talking… to myself." Her tone was heavy with embarrassment. "It is a bad habit, and if I think about it, I can stop, but I don't think about it often and…"

Her simple confession caught him off guard. Laughter rumbled from his core. He couldn't remember the last time he'd laughed like this. It felt good.

"And what do you find so amusing?" With her hands on her hips, she looked like a little girl scolding her brother.

"You. One moment you are talking to yourself, and the next you are babbling."

She eyed him with contempt before breaking into laughter, too.

What was it about her? He was angry and disgusted by her father's underhanded actions, and had all but convinced himself she was part of her father's scheme. But she had never asked or demanded anything of him. He was attracted to her, but did not want anything to do with her. She'd infiltrated his house, won the respect of his servants, and yet, he still could not escape all his doubts. His emotions were as different as night and day.

The silence grew between them. This was not progressing well. He did not want to blurt out his plan. He wanted—no, needed—her cooperation. He knew he was trapped.

His goal was to win his aunt's approval and survive Christmastide. And, since he'd been forced into marriage, he might as well make the best of the situation. At least his aunt and grandmother couldn't nag him about his marital status anymore. They need never know the truth.

Wiping her hands down her apron, she inquired, "Did you want to speak with me about something?"

"As a matter of fact, there is a matter we need to discuss."

She stopped what she was doing. Her face remained emotionless, but Marcus could see every muscle in her body had tensed.

"My aunt has arrived and intends to spend the holiday with us." Her mouth opened, but before she could speak, he added, "I have a proposition."

FAITH DID NOT KNOW what she had expected to hear, but the arrival of his aunt was the last thing she would have ever guessed. When they married, Lord Hawthorne had made it perfectly clear that she was not to make herself known to anyone, and that he had no intention of revealing the news to his family. She had wondered how long he would be able to keep it a secret. The marriage of a marquess to anyone was bound to create a stir.

His next sentence was even more of a shock. "She is under the impression that we married for love."

Faith could not believe her ears. She fumbled with the words, "Why does she…" The guilty look on Lord Hawthorne's face answered her unfinished question. He reminded her of a little boy who was desperately trying to get himself out of the trouble he should never have got himself into in the first place. "Why did you tell her that?"

He ran a large hand through his golden locks, his eyes narrowed and jaw clenched. She knew *that* look. Her pulse quickened, and she took a step back.

He was silent for the longest time before his features finally relaxed. He took in a deep breath. "The reason is of no consequence. I need you to pretend to be a loving wife."

She should have known better than to challenge him, but

curiosity got the better of her. "I think I should know the reason. How else am I to pretend?" The moment she heard the questioning tone in her own voice, she knew she had overstepped boundaries.

"This is my house, my family." His voice pulsated more with frustration than anger, but it had the same effect on her none-the-less.

She backed away until she bumped into the table. She was cornered. Lord Hawthorne's harsh tone had reached the very core of her being. She fought to maintain her composure, and to not crumple under the table. She closed her eyes, hoping this would soon come to an end, but her body started to tremble and beads of perspiration formed on her brow. The horrible feeling in her gut grew stronger and stronger. *Please don't hurt me.* She wanted to scream. She wanted to…

A soft hand cradled her cheek, and a gentle voice called her back to the present. "Shh, it's all right."

She stood still for a long time. She was afraid to open her eyes, that it was a cruel joke. It had been such a long time since she'd been comforted. He stroked her cheek once again before removing his hand.

When at last she did open her eyes, his gaze was one of concern. She couldn't explain it, but in that moment, some-thing changed between them.

In slow measures, her breathing returned to normal. She did not want to lie, but the truth was even more distressing. "I'm sorry. Ever since that night at the inn…"

Shaking his head, Lord Hawthorne said, "You do not need to explain. I should not have lost my temper." He inhaled deeply, then, on a long slow exhale, continued, "I am the one who should be apologizing to you. I have been out of sorts of late."

But it was *her* fault he was out of sorts. Trying to regain her composure, she blinked away the remaining tears, cleared her voice, and sidestepped him, creating distance. Bringing him back to the topic at hand, she reminded him, "You mentioned a proposition."

He appeared lost in thought before blurting out his scheme. "I need to convince my aunt that I am happily married. If you act the part of the loving wife, you may remain at Deer Park and do as you please—providing there is no scandal—and I will continue to live in London."

Faith had once dreamed of love and a happy marriage, but her fantasy had changed. These past months had been peaceful, and she felt safe here. Dreams of love had been pushed aside for safety and security. Living at Deer Park was more than she could have hoped for. There had been no fighting, and no….

She swallowed hard. "How am I supposed to convince your aunt?"

The longer he looked at her, the more her heart pounded. She didn't know if it was from fear or… Foreign pleasant tingles started to bubble within. *Oh dear.* Why did he continue to stare? She did not know how long she could maintain her composure.

"Well…" He appeared just as unsure about how to create a loving marriage as she was.

She did not know anything about his parents, only that they had died when he was young. As with most marriages of the *ton*, his parents' union had probably not been a happy one.

"Well," he started once again, "You could use my given name, offer smiles, and…" His words trailed as he ran a frustrated hand through his hair.

"I do not even know your given name." She knew he had an array of titles and names, but had never referred to him as anything but Lord Hawthorne.

He took a step back, bowed playfully, and said, "Marcus,

at your service, my lady." She could not help but giggle. This side of him was so different from that which she was used to seeing. "And you are?"

She curtseyed. "Faith. Pleased to meet you, my lord." He raised a brow in correction. "Marcus." Another giggle escaped her lips, and the tension she had been feeling since his arrival eased.

After the initial awkwardness had worn off, they passed a most pleasant hour. Marcus walked with her back toward the house, pointing out his favorite childhood haunts. They turned the corner and the sound of a dog barking got closer and closer.

"Balder, no…" Faith cried. But before she could finish her sentence, Balder charged at Marcus, knocking him to the ground. The dog snarled at him while his large front paws on Marcus' chest kept him in a prone position.

"I believe my dog is under the impression that you need protecting."

Faith started to laugh at the dog's attempt at chivalry. "Balder is a most gallant knight, indeed."

Faith could not remember ever being so nervous in her entire life. The afternoon had ended on such a positive note, but now all the anxiety was back… tenfold. How did one go about pretending to be happily married?

Pausing in front of one of the gilded mirrors adorned with a swag of holly in the hall, she answered her own question. "I suppose I should smile and compliment him."

Walking down the hall, she attempted to distract mind from all the nervous energy coursing through her body, glancing about, admiring how well the decorations looked. The spicy scents of rosemary and pine drifted through the air. It had been quite the task to decorate such a large home, but she had enjoyed every minute of it.

The red salon was where the family gathered before dinner, or so she'd been informed. She had seen this room for all of two minutes when Caspar had given her a tour of the house upon her arrival, but she'd had no reason to use it since. Over the past months, she had kept no company, and it had not even dawned on her to decorate this room for the season. Thankfully, one of the staff had added a few holiday embellishments.

As she walked into the opulent space, she breathed a sigh of relief. She was the first to arrive. She took the opportunity to absorb the sophisticated details all around. The rich hue of claret, the gilded furniture, and the centuries-old portraits on the wall were all most intimidating. Even though her father had made quite a fortune in trade, his house was nothing compared to this. She walked to the black- and-white marble mantel, admiring the bust of Apollo, when a deep, familiar voice sent a pleasant shiver down her spine.

"Good evening, my dear."

She turned at the sound of Marcus' voice, and her heart nearly stopped at the handsome figure he cut. All words caught in her throat. She did not know how she managed it, but somehow, she muttered out, "Happy Christmas."

He strolled up to her, clearly at ease amongst all this elegance. "Relax," he whispered into her ear.

She tried, but to no avail. Her nerves were strung too tight. She did not know how she would get through this evening. The butterflies in her stomach only increased when Lady Hawthorne walked through the door.

Marcus greeted the older woman and then turned to Faith. "May I introduce you to my aunt, Lady Hawth—"

Lady Hawthorne pushed her nephew aside with a wave of her hand and stepped closer. After being under her scrutinizing eye for several seconds, his aunt finally spoke to her. "You're quite lovely. I have a sense about these things. My nephew chose well. You may call me Aunt Lou. We do not need to be so formal here." Her sentences were quick, to the point, and spoken with kindness. Faith liked her instantly.

Pleasantries were passed back and forth, and before too long, dinner was announced.

Marcus escorted his aunt into the dining room, and Faith followed close behind. The smell of roasted boar wafted through the air. A fanciful feast was laid out before them.

Throughout dinner, Faith watched as Marcus and his aunt chatted. Their casual conversation created a relaxed atmosphere. Not even the intrusion of Balder, who crept under the table and settled by Faith's feet, disrupted the delightful evening.

"I understand that you decorated the house for Advent." Faith braced herself for a scolding from Aunt Lou. Marchionesses most likely did not climb ladders or toil with greenery. "The house looks lovely." Aunt Lou's praise warmed her heart.

By the time dinner ended, Faith was much more at ease.

Aunt Lou led the way back to the red salon. Marcus offered his arm to Faith. No sooner had she accepted than Balder took his place on the other side of her.

"I believe I have lost my dog forever."

Heat rose up her cheeks. "I am so sorry, I didn't…"

Marcus leaned in and whispered, "I'm teasing." As the words brushed her cheek, her heart skipped a beat. She was enjoying this side of him. Too much, perhaps.

Feeling more confident, she decided to rib him back. "Perhaps if you bribed him…" She stopped short when Aunt Lou turned around and eyed her and Marcus for a long moment.

Wondering if she had spilled something on her dress, she

followed Aunt Lou's gaze, but when it travelled upward, she swallowed hard. *Mistletoe*. The pounding in her chest grew louder and louder as she wondered what Marcus would do.

The decision was made for him.

"Kiss her," Aunt Lou commanded, rather than stated, with a playful smile. Faith looked at him with uncertainty. *Was this a test?* They had never exchanged a kiss, not even after their hasty marriage. And the few times when he'd visited, he'd been here so briefly that she'd never had the chance to get to know him, let alone share intimacies.

Marcus took one step in, and her pulse started to hammer in rhythm with her heart. She felt anxious and a little light-headed, although not in a bad way, just not in the way she was used to feeling when the opposite sex was near. He didn't say a word but bent his head and gave her a kiss on the mouth.

When their lips met, her world became brighter, and a tingling sensation replaced her anxious anticipation. His lips were soft and gentle, and he tasted like sweet custard. She was flying on a cloud of mistletoe across a snowy landscape. She had never been so aware of him as she was now.

She did not know if he felt the same way. She assumed not. Marcus was handsome and probably had his fair share of female attention. What was she to him but an inconvenience, his unwanted bride?

Disappointment rushed through her when the kiss ended, and Marcus stepped back. He did not say a word to her. He turned to his aunt, bid her good night, and left the room, leaving a very puzzled Faith to wonder what she had done wrong.

The next words only added to her misery. "I suppose this is the perfect opportunity to get to know one another," his aunt said in a cheerful voice.

Faith's stomach plunged. She had hoped that when

Marcus' aunt interrogated her about their marriage, he would at least be present to offer some support. It was not in her nature to lie, and besides, she was not very good at it.

Aunt Lou sat on the elegant damask settee and patted her hand on the plump red cushion. "Come, sit with me."

Faith perched on the edge of the seat and clasped her hands in her lap. Balder followed her and rested his head beside her hands, clearly wanting affection.

"Tell me about your family."

She did not want Marcus' aunt to think less of her because of her simple upbringing. The world of her youth had been vastly different to the one she now resided in. She swallowed hard. "My mother died in childbirth when I was just a few years old. After she died, my father was heartbroken. He was gone an awful lot. His investments prospered and…"

We were happier when he was not around.

"Do you have any siblings?"

A hard lump formed in her throat. "I had an older sister, but she died."

"Oh, it must have been awful to lose a sister. What happened?" Aunt Lou's probing did not bother her. The older woman was not judging or condescending in her questioning, but seemed to take a genuine interest in Faith's life.

"I really don't remember much." She had been barely ten years old when the accident occurred. All she remembered was that one day her sister was healthy, and the next, Mary was battered and bruised. "She said she fell from a horse."

Aunt Lou's grey eyebrows joined together, her expression turned to one of confusion. "You didn't know anything had happened?"

"No, I didn't. I wasn't allowed to see her, and then when I did…" Angry, muted screams penetrated to the forefront of her consciousness, and she rubbed her temples as recollections of that stormy day threatened her present. "I…I don't know… but…" She met Aunt Lou's eyes. "I don't ever recall her riding." The confession passed her lips a mere whisper. She didn't want to think about that day, about what had actually happened.

Aunt Lou patted her hand. "The mind helps us to forget painful memories."

Faith did not know if she entirely believed Aunt Lou's theory, but her kind gesture was much appreciated. However, she did not want to delve further into her upbringing. She would rather spend the time learning about her husband.

"What was Marcus like as a boy?"

Aunt Lou's face brightened. "He was such a mischievous little boy, always getting into or climbing onto something. He never could stay in one spot for long."

An image of a blond-haired little boy climbing trees or sneaking sweets from the kitchen emerged. "He must have been such a happy child."

"He was, until…" Aunt Lou frowned, her tone turned somber. "He may raise his voice and may be quick to anger, but it is only his way of protecting his heart. Give him time."

Faith was beginning to understand why Marcus often lost his temper. She suspected he was just a scared little boy on the inside, who had been hurt and was in desperate need of love.

CHAPTER 5

"Good afternoon, Lady Hawthorne." The sweet sound of the familiar voice was a soothing balm to her frayed nerves. The torrent of emotions she had experienced over the past twenty-four hours had been overwhelming.

"Happy Christmas, Mrs. Gardner." Faith had come to enjoy her time with the widow, who had no children or grandchildren of her own to pass the time with.

Although Mrs. Gardner was old enough to be Faith's mother, the two had become instant friends after literally bumping into each other at the drapers. They had chatted for quite some time, and in the end, Mrs. Gardner had offered to aid Faith in setting the orangery to rights. She had even shared some stories of the previous Lord and Lady Hawthorne, which Faith was most grateful to hear. Over the course of the past few months, their friendship had grown and Faith cherished it. True friends were far and few between in her life.

"How are you enjoying yourself this Christmastide?"

"Lord Hawthorne arrived…" Mrs. Gardner went rigid,

her face pale. Faith put her hand on the lady's shoulder. "Are you unwell?"

The widow cleared her throat and offered reassurances. "Perfectly. I just… thought of something that needs to be tended to later." Finding sudden interest in a small lemon tree, she prompted Faith to continue, "You were saying?"

"Oh, yes, Lord Hawthorne arrived on Boxing Day." She left out the parts about their argument, her unsuccessful attempt at running away, her bargain with Marcus, and their first kiss. The latter had caused her the most confusion.

With an air of nonchalance, Mrs. Gardner stated over her shoulder, "I had not heard that Lord Hawthorne was expected."

Faith was certain that Mrs. Gardner was hiding something, but despite her curiosity, she did not want to pry. "He did not send word beforehand." The words came out in a mere whisper. She did not want to admit that they had not been in communication prior to Marcus' unexpected arrival.

"What happened, my dear?"

She must have been wearing her emotions on her sleeve again. It was a bad habit, and one she truly should attempt to overcome. Although the weight of her ordeal was bearing down on her, and she wanted to confide in someone, there were certain things she did not want to discuss. Avoiding the heart of the issue, she decided to move to a different topic. "How do you know when you're in love?"

Her stomach churned when Mrs. Gardner let out a small laugh. She knew it was a naïve question. But she was curious. How would she know if she was in love with her husband? She found him handsome, and he'd saved her from a dreadful existence, but that wasn't love. Or was that part of it? She truly didn't know. And even if she *was* in love with her husband, what could she offer him in return? Matters of the heart were quite confusing.

"Oh, my little dear," Mrs. Gardner said as she embraced Faith. "Falling in love can be the most wonderful feeling in the entire world. Your heart beats faster and you can't wait to be with him."

Mrs. Gardner's enthusiasm for the topic gave Faith hope, but it still didn't answer all her questions. "But how do you know when he feels the same?"

"Give him time. His childhood was not always a happy one."

Faith's heart ached for her husband. How sad he must have been at times without a mother, and a father who rarely gave him attention. Their situations were similar in a way, but Faith, at the very least, had a sister who'd loved her, if only for a brief time.

Mary had often created fanciful tales where Faith was the heroine and her true love saved her from an evil villain. Those were always Faith's favorite stories.

"Was it love at first sight with Mr. Gardner?"

Mrs. Gardner's eyes filled with sadness, sorrow weighing down her features.

"I'm sorry, I should not have…"

Shaking her head, Mrs. Gardner corrected her. "It is not your fault."

Sadness struck her heart as a hard lump formed in her throat. She felt sorry for the lonely woman, who must still miss her late husband terribly.

Changing the topic of conversation, Mrs. Gardner walked over to the hothouse roses and began to clip the dead leaves away. "What would you like to plant this spring?"

"I haven't given it much consideration, but I do love flowers and…" Faith continued to blather on about her favorite blooms and colors while tending to the small lemon tree.

. . .

FOR THE SECOND time since he'd returned home, Marcus found himself reluctantly trudging his way to the orangery. When he entered the warm space, the sweet scent of lilac teased his senses, reminding him of a distant memory.

Why did Faith like this place so much?

Faith's back was toward him. The simple sky-blue morning dress that she wore accentuated her delicate curves. Marcus could have watched her for hours, but there were more pressing matters to deal with.

"…but my absolute favorite is the damask rose, and…"

"Talking to yourself again?"

She jumped. "Oh… I did not hear you enter. No, I was just…" She glanced around as if she'd lost something.

"Talking to yourself," he teased.

"I suppose I am," she said with a giggle.

Marcus walked up to his wife and handed her a letter. "This just arrived from your father."

She looked down at the envelope in his hand as if he were attempting to hand her a death sentence. All the color drained from her face and her tear-filled eyes met his. Her breath came in short, shaky spurts. "I don't want… Please don't make me see him."

Marcus took a step closer, and she backed away. He hadn't noticed it before, but now it was obvious that she was afraid of her father. Why? When he'd first met them both at the theatre, they'd appeared to have an amiable father-daughter relationship.

She continued to stare at the envelope, refusing to even touch it.

He tried to coax an answer from her. "Why don't you want to see him?"

She took another step backwards, putting more distance between them. "I just don't. Please don't make me," she pleaded.

"If you would just…"

"I can't," she cried before running out of the orangery.

FAITH HAD SENT word that she was retiring for the evening with a headache, which caused Marcus great concern. He wanted to go to her and demand that she tell him what was wrong, and why she was so distraught about receiving a letter from her father. In the end, it was Aunt Lou who convinced him to have patience.

To make matters worse, the untimely arrival of Artemisia and Nigel, and the unexpected addition of Artemisia's niece, Mathilda, forced Marcus to play host for the evening. However, even with all the distractions, he could not forget the conversation he'd had with Faith earlier in the day.

It wasn't until everyone had retired for the night that Marcus was able to give more consideration to his situation with her. Every time her father was mentioned, her countenance changed to one of despair. He had also noticed that she became skittish around all the male servants, too, save Caspar. And as for when he'd lost his temper on the night of his return, well…

The pieces of the puzzle were slowly coming together, and he did not like the image he saw. Whitworth would not harm his own daughter, would he? Just the thought of the man striking Faith made his blood boil. He himself might speak harshly or lose his temper at times, but he would never physically take his anger out on a woman.

Crossing the length of his chamber, he went to the cabinet and pulled a glass and a bottle of brandy from its dark interior. He poured a healthy helping of the amber liquid. *Damn to these feelings*, he toasted silently before swallowing the warming spirit.

He was about to pour another glass when a muffled cry sounded from the marchioness' suite.

Marcus stood still, holding his breath. Nothing.

Was he imagining cries in the night?

Putting down the bottle and empty glass, he went to investigate. Something nagged at his conscience. Something seemed… not quite right. He strode to the door that separated their rooms. Without knocking, he opened it slightly. Another soft cry met his ears.

"Don't hurt me," he thought he heard a soft voice cry.

Without a second thought, he stormed into Faith's bedroom, his heart pounding against his chest. He did not know what he was expecting to find, but all he saw was his wife, sound asleep, the only sound coming from the crackle and hiss of the dying embers in the fireplace. Their faint glow cast eerie shadows upon the walls.

Suddenly murmurs from beyond the shadows broke through the silence. He stepped closer to the bed.

"Don't hurt me." Faith's cries grew louder. Her body thrashed as if she was trying to get away from some unseen demon. "Father, no, please, no…" Her words died on a sob.

Marcus rubbed the back of his neck. His fears were confirmed. He did not want to wake her, only to offer comfort. Sitting down and stroking her damp hair, he cooed, "Shh, it's all right." Her body tossed from side to side, as if trapped between two worlds.

He climbed into the bed, settling beside her. He ran his hand over her back. "Shh, I won't let him harm you."

She was his responsibility now, and he would ensure that no harm *ever* came to her. Several moments passed before her breathing evened out, and her features had relaxed. Wrapping his arms about her, he brought her in closer to him, desperate to keep the demons away.

"You're safe now," he whispered.

CHAPTER 6

Faith's head rose, then fell gently back onto a pillow of safety and warmth. The scents of pine and leather invaded her dreams, and strong arms nestled her in a warm cocoon. *Strong arms?* Her heart beat quickened as realization dawned that she was not alone. Her eyes opened wide, trying to take in her surroundings. She pushed herself off the cotton-clad chest. Breathing heavily, she stared down into concerned honey eyes.

Why was Marcus in her bed? Was he here to claim his husbandly rights? Her mind raced with the possibilities.

She struggled to move away from him, but he wrapped a gentle arm around her and brought her back down onto his chest. "Shh, I'm not going to hurt you." His voice was soft… caring. He ran his hand through her hair, smoothing the tangled strands. Her breathing eased with each gentle stroke, and her body relaxed. She felt him kiss the top of her head, and closing her eyes, relished the soothing aura he created around her. It was a pleasant experience, one that she had never felt before.

"Just rest," he cooed.

The morning sun peeked through the heavy curtains. She rubbed her cheek against the softness of Marcus' shirt. Her body tingled with each breath she took. It was far too easy to lose herself in the comfort of his arms.

Wondering how long he'd been in her bed, she worked up the courage to ask him, whispering against his chest, "What are you doing here?"

"You were having a nightmare."

The breath left her body. *Please don't ask*, she chanted in her head. She did not want to talk about it. She wasn't ready to tell him. He had shown her kindness, and whenever he was near, her insides bubbled with excitement, but that did not mean she could trust him with her secret

He would be appalled and disgusted.

She looked up and met his gaze. "It was nothing."

He raised a skeptical brow.

Thinking quickly, she decided to share what he already knew and hoped that would suffice for the meantime. Her words sounded broken, strangled. "Images from that night at the inn often come back and haunt me." It was the truth, but there was more… too much more. She swallowed hard, past the aching lump in her throat. "Nothing more."

"I hope you know you are safe here. Safe with me." There was no hint of inconvenience or disdain in his tone, only a sincere declaration that caught her completely off guard.

Faith raised her head and looked into those perfect honey-colored eyes. She felt like he just handed her the world. "Thank you."

"LADY HAWTHORNE, I have a message from Lord Hawthorne." Caspar approached before Faith reached her destination.

"Lord Hawthorne has been detained on estate business and will join you shortly in the day parlor."

When Marcus informed her that more of his family had arrived, she had wanted to bury her head under the blanket and sleep through the winter. But marchionesses did not have that luxury. They were supposed to be composed and confident. They were expected to be proper hostesses—be welcoming and smile at their guests. Marcus had said he would be right by her side, and now she was to meet his relatives on her own?

She intertwined her fingers to stop them from trembling, and they turned white with the pressure. "Thank you, Caspar," she managed to say through gulps of air. He gave her a reassuring smile before taking his leave.

"I can do this," she mumbled under her breath. She checked her hair once more in the gilded mirror. Troth had made her look the part of a marchioness, but on the inside, she was still just the daughter of a tradesman, and as inexperienced and unsure as any simple country girl.

Taking deep breaths to steady her breathing, she edged her way to the parlor.

Faint sounds of laughter met her ears. Her stomach tightened and knotted with each step. She sucked in her breath and stepped into the bright day parlor. All eyes immediately turned to her.

Silence.

Somewhere deep in the house, a faint tick-tock resonated.

A thousand and one notions whipped through her mind. She wondered if they had discovered that Marcus had been forced to marry her, and that was why they all were silent. She desperately wanted to retreat. She took one step back. The sound of her own breathing, which came in short spurts, was in rhythm with the quivering lancing through

her body. She wished someone would say something…
anything.

"You're quite lovely." She looked down at the smiling
child, who had to be no more than six. "You can sit with me,"
the rosy-cheeked, bright-eyed girl said as she took Faith's
hand and pulled her toward an unoccupied settee. "My name
is Mathilda, but everyone calls me Mat. That is Aunt
Artemisia, but I call her Aunt Arte." The young child did not
let anyone else speak. Pointing to the attractive man sitting
next to her aunt, she continued, "This is Uncle Nigel." She
leaned in close to Faith and whispered none too softly, "Aunt
Arte almost didn't marry him because he is a rake."

"Mat!" Aunt Lou scolded.

"It is true, Aunt Lou," the little girl declared with empha-
sis. "Mama said so."

Faith could not stop the giggle from exiting her mouth.
Within moments, the entire room was filled with laughter.
The tension she had been feeling began to dissolve.

Nigel then stood and said in a teasing tone, "As much as I
would love to stay and hear how my darling wife almost did
not marry me, I believe more manly pursuits are in order.
I'm off to discover where Marcus is hiding."

"Did I just hear my name?"

"Marcus!" Mat squealed with delight, hopping off the
settee and running into his open embrace.

Faith's heart skipped a beat at the sight of her husband
strolling into the day parlor clad in buff riding breeches and
a hunter green coat, looking relaxed, at ease. It reminded her
of the first night they met.

"What are you up to, little hoyden?" Marcus picked Mat
up, tickling her. The child's sweet giggles were contagious. It
was such a precious sight to see her husband interacting with
the little girl.

With Mat still in his arms, Marcus turned to Faith, his

warm smile taking her breath away. "And how are you faring this morning, my dear?"

My dear. She knew it was a charade, but her heart melted just the same. *Don't raise your hopes.* She reminded herself. After Twelfth Night, Marcus would return to London, and she would once again be alone.

When she'd first agreed to his bargain, she had not minded the prospect of residing at Deer Park without him. But with each kind word and gentle touch, she was losing her heart to him.

Before she could respond, Aunt Lou offered a smile to her and then scolded Marcus with a playful goad. "Really, Marcus, she is doing very well. You act as if we're ogres. Now, if you and Nigel will so kindly leave us be, we have more important matters to discuss."

Mat squirmed out of Marcus' embrace and joined Faith on the settee. Marcus sauntered over to Faith, leaned in, and whispered, "Have fun, my dear," before brushing a soft kiss on her cheek.

She looked into those honey eyes and felt herself drowning in their sweetness. In that moment, the curtain dropped; she could no longer pretend, could no longer deny her feelings. She held her breath, unable to speak, but offered a smile as he took his leave. He appeared just as discomposed as she was.

The moment Nigel and Marcus were clear of the room, Artemisia clasped her hands together and declared, "Now that my husband is out of the way, we can discuss more important matters."

Beaming, Mat clarified the situation for Faith. "It is a tradition that the ladies plan Twelfth Night, and this year Aunt Lou said I was old enough to help."

Artemisia presented the first idea. "I think we should play bullet pudding. It is always great fun." Her bright smile lit up the room as she giggled. "Do you remember the last time we played? It was when Phil caught the attention of Mr. Buttress?"

Aunt Lou laughed. "Unwanted attention, that is. She spent most of the evening trying to avoid him and missed out on the sugar cakes."

Faith sat back and listened to the exchange. A small part of her was envious. They appeared to be such a loving family. She'd always longed to be part of a family. *Perhaps one day...*

"What do you think we should do, Faith?"

She was so unnerved by Artemisia's question that she could not speak for several seconds. No one ever asked her opinion.

Once again, it was Mat who eased her nervousness. "You don't have to worry about Aunt Arte, she won't bite."

As if believing he might be the topic of conversation, Balder strolled in and nuzzled against Faith's dove-colored skirt. Mat slid off the settee none too delicately, as only a young child could, and showered the dog with affection.

Faith glanced over to Artemisia and saw the sincerity in her expression. She had never experienced such kindness in her entire life as she had these past months at Deer Park. Worrying her lower lip, she thought for a moment, then shyly said, "I've always loved playacting."

"That is an excellent idea!" Aunt Lou began with as much excitement as a child. "We have not put on a play in years. I'll ask Thomas to bring down the old trunks from the attic. Combined with the costumes from Knollwood, we should have plenty to work with."

The remainder of the afternoon was spent organizing costumes and listening to Aunt Lou share stories of when her nieces and nephews were little.

Although Faith missed her sister, it was good to be part of a family again, even if only for a short time.

"I HAVE to say I am shocked that you got yourself leg-shackled," Nigel chaffed as they rode side by side.

Marcus did not appreciate the hint of laughter in his best friend's tone. It was none of his business what he decided to do or with whom.

"Artemisia would be angry if she heard you refer to marriage in such a way." Marcus thought his comeback was weak at best. He'd never been one to think of witty responses on the spur of the moment.

Nigel pulled his horse to a stop and glared. His question was straight to the point. "When are you going to tell me what this is all about?"

"What is there to explain?" Marcus started to edge his horse forward, but Nigel reached out and grabbed the leather bridle, bringing him to a halt once again.

"You once helped me to see the errors of my ways. I intend to do the same for you. What's going on?"

"Married less than a year and already an expert?"

"That's what being happily married to the woman you love does to you." Nigel's smug response struck a chord with Marcus. His friend's eyes narrowed. His tone was deep and forceful. "What *is* going on?"

He had never heard Nigel use such a firm tone.

Letting out a long breath, Marcus began, "Do you remember that night at the theatre when Lady Jefferson was seen leaving in the company of that tradesman and then all the gossip that followed?"

"The *ton* still holds that indiscretion against her. She has not been seen in polite society since. What does that have to do with your marriage, though?"

"The man she left with is Faith's father. Lady Jefferson had introduced us only a couple of hours previous."

Nigel shook his head. "I am still not understanding what all that has to do with your marriage."

"Don't you find it odd that Lady Jefferson introduced me to Faith and her father, and then the following night I found myself rescuing Faith from an assailant, only to be forced to the altar?"

"Where were you when you rescued her?"

The sharp, clipped tone of Marcus' voice was laced with annoyance. "I was staying at The Running Stag on my way here when I came across Faith and her father."

"Just a coincidence. You are deluded."

Nigel's slowness at comprehending the situation aggravated Marcus.

"Very few people knew I was leaving town, but Lady Jefferson did. After the fact, I discovered Faith's father wanted connections to the *ton,* and what better way to achieve that end than to have his daughter marry someone with a title?"

"Let me see if I understand this correctly. You believe that Faith's father arranged for her to seduce you at the coaching inn?" Nigel's voice was heavy with skepticism.

Perhaps if Marcus had not lived through it, he would feel the same.

"Not seduce." This was the part that was difficult to explain. Under normal circumstances, Marcus would have found the look of utter bewilderment on Nigel's face most entertaining, but there was nothing amusing about the situation. "She was being attacked, and I rescued her. Her dress was torn, and her father thought I had compromised her."

"What sort of father would have his daughter...?" The

words hung in the air as understanding set in. "You believe your wife to be part of the scheme."

"Yes… no… I don't know."

Marcus still did not understand what had happened at The Running Stag, but every instinct told him that his wife was an innocent pawn in a dangerous game that her father had played. The more time he spent with her, the more she affected him. He did not know why he'd kissed her cheek in the parlor. It had been a spontaneous action, and one he'd enjoyed more than he was willing to admit.

Damn these emotions.

Marcus dismounted and tied his horse to a low-hanging branch. Within moments, Nigel had done the same and was walking beside him.

"You mean to tell me that you allowed yourself to be taken in by this bastard and his whore of a daughter?"

Without thinking, Marcus swung his fist, making contact with Nigel's jaw. The other man's head whipped back to one side. "Don't you ever call her that," Marcus' voice rumbled through the calm countryside.

Ridding himself of the effects of Marcus' punch, Nigel rubbed his face. "I suppose you don't believe her to be part of her father's scheme, after all."

Stretching his fingers, Marcus stepped in and shook his head. "I'm sorry… I have been…" Pushing his fist into his other hand, he continued, "I just needed to hit something."

"The next time you decide to take your anger out on someone, let's find a more deserving victim."

Marcus laughed and slapped Nigel's back. "I believe you had it coming for causing Artemisia such grief."

∼

LATER THAT EVENING, after dinner, everyone adjourned to the Stone Hall. The Yule Log had been lit days before and was still providing warmth. A hint of clove wafted through the air, adding to the cozy environment.

Mathilda wanted to recite her poem about the Yule Log, and Artemisia promised to sing for everyone if Aunt Lou entertained them on the pianoforte. All Marcus wanted to do was to be alone with his wife.

Faith stood to one side, seemingly lost in her own thoughts. He couldn't keep his eyes off her. She was wearing a silk dress in that same shade of blue that deepened the color of her eyes. Blue ribbons danced through her light blonde hair. She looked like an angel at night. Except he was fairly certain most angels did not have their own furry guardian.

Balder was lying at her feet, watching his every move. Marcus did not know what possessed him, but he had an intense urge to be near her that was almost overwhelming. The dog raised his head but did not snarl or growl as he approached.

Faith edged back a couple of steps. She appeared nervous. There was a pang in his heart as his chest constricted. She still did not have confidence in him. After what he suspected, he couldn't blame her. He was more determined than ever to win her trust.

Marcus leaned his head in and kissed her cheek. "You're standing under the mistletoe." He stepped back and held out his hand. Her eyes shone brightly, her cheeks blushed. "May I have this dance?"

He heard Artemisia sigh. "How sweet."

Marcus cared naught for the opinions of others. He was not putting on an act. The charade had long since ended. He wanted to spend time with his wife, get to know his wife, to dance with his wife. If it were up to him, he would order everyone else out of Deer Park.

Faith was slow to accept. She worried her bottom lip as she placed her petite hand in his. He could feel her pulse quicken through her gloves as he guided her to the center of the room. He placed his hand on her tiny waist and began to hum.

Within seconds of their movement, Aunt Lou had begun to play a melodious waltz on the pianoforte.

SHIMMERING gold ribbons danced in the candlelight, and warmth from the Yule Log cascaded and swirled about the space.

Ever since that first night when they were introduced at the theatre in London, Faith had dreamed of a moment like this. Despite Marcus' temper, she was drawn to him. She no longer feared his dark moods and hoped with time and love, they would ease. Something deep inside told her she *could* trust him.

When Marcus took her hand, that bubbling feeling she'd felt that first night when they'd met came back tenfold. She looked away, afraid he might sense her feelings.

Marcus squeezed her hand. "You need not be shy around me." Her world tipped upside down at the husky tone in his voice. She suspected he was flirting with her, and the thought thrilled her through and through.

The moment the chords of the waltz began, the Stone Hall magically transformed into a winter fantasy that existed for just the two of them. No longer was the room just a grand space of stark white marble, but a snowy landscape decorated in varying hues of green. The smell of fresh evergreen infiltrated her senses. She looked into Marcus' honey-colored eyes, wanting to drink in their sweet nectar.

Marcus brought her body in closer to his. His strong thigh guided her into the next twirl. She swayed into the movements, hoping this was not a dream, hoping this would never end, hoping...

The music softened her soul and allowed her to experience emotions she never thought possible. Every inch of her tingled and was flooded with warmth. She wanted Marcus to hold her like this forever.

But when the music began to fade, she flittered back to reality. Marcus brushed a soft kiss across her cheek; his lips were warm, his breathing uneven. When their eyes met, the glint in his eyes told her he'd enjoyed their dance as much as she had. The attraction was undeniable, and the sensations lasted throughout the evening. Every time Faith glanced Marcus' way, his eyes were soft with an emotion that she could not name but made her weak at the knees.

The evening progressed in pleasant measures. Mathilda recited her poem, and Artemisia sang several Italian love songs.

When it was time to retire, Faith did not know what to make of Marcus' presence beside her as they climbed the stairs toward the marquess and marchioness' suite. On previous evenings, she had retired to her room while Marcus retreated to his study. Was this to be the night that he claimed his husbandly rights? Her pulse thrummed and her legs felt as if they shook with each step. It wasn't that she did not want to be his wife in full, but she was nervous.

By the time they reached the marchioness' rooms, the fear of the unknown had all but consumed her, shattering her nerves into shards of broken glass.

"May I join you?"

She could feel the heat rise in her cheeks with his words. This *was* to be the night. The shock and anxiety must have shown on her face.

She swallowed hard, but before she could respond, he quickly added, "I just want to spend time with you."

She looked into the depths of those honey-colored eyes she was coming to adore. She thought back to the previous night. He had not pressed his advantage when she'd had the nightmare. Quite the contrary, in fact. She nodded her head in acquiescence, still unsure, but willing to take a chance.

He opened the door to her private sitting room and stepped aside. She entered the warm rose-pink space and walked to the crimson velvet settee, continuing to take long, deep breaths. Vanilla and lavender wafted through the air, helping to ease—a little at least—the tension of the unknown.

She sat down, her back straight and fingers intertwined, unsure what was to come next. He took the seat across from her. "Faith, relax. You have no need to fear me." His tone was gentle, the words thoughtful and tender. "I just want to get to know you better, and for you to know me. Nothing more."

She curved her back into the soft fabric and let out a deep sigh.

They sat in awkward silence for several long seconds. Uncertain if he expected her to begin the conversation, she broached a topic she was curious about. "Your aunt told me you and Nigel were partners in mischief while growing up."

Marcus' robust laughter filled the dainty confines of her room. "That is quite the understatement. My aunt had a difficult time taming us."

Faith joined in his laughter. She loved hearing happy stories about family—*his* family.

"We were always off on some grand adventure, traversing the vastness of Knollwood, usually ending with us covered in dirt and mud, and beyond recognition." Playfully teasing, Marcus raised a questioning brow, and stated, "I am most certain that you never got into any mischief."

Biting her lower lip to control her creeping smile, she shook her head. "No, never. My sister was the impish one, mostly in the form of sneaking sweets from the kitchen."

She was surprised how easily the words flowed. The hours flew past in blissful reminiscence as each shared tales and adventures from childhood. As dawn approached, the beginning of the new day—a new world—made itself known. And without a doubt, she had fallen in love with her husband.

CHAPTER 7

An uneventful day had come and gone. Darkness consumed the land. The clock in the main hall chimed eleven. The hour was late by country standards. Marcus could not escape thoughts of Faith. His family had adapted easily—too easily—to her presence. Gulping down the last of the amber liquid, he slammed the glass on the desk.

Damn, what was it about her he could not resist? He had no need for a wife. He did not need that complication in his life. He would have been perfectly content letting the title, and all the headaches associated with it, pass to one of his cousins. He could have denied marrying her, paid off her father. But for the life of him, he hadn't been able to say no.

Ever since the first night when they'd met, he had not thought of anyone else. Even after they were married and she came to Deer Park while he returned to London, he could not escape the thought of her. She consumed his waking moments and haunted his dreams. Her sweet nature and commitment to her role as marchioness almost made him believe that anything was possible.

He had written to his steward often, inquiring how she faired. The response made him even more agitated. The staff loved her, and the tenants adored her. She was like a bright star on a dark and dreary evening. Even his dog had chosen her over him.

Marcus took the steps two at a time. He did not want to disturb her, only to ensure her safety, he told himself. Reaching the landing to the family wing, he assured himself that it was only natural for a husband to want to protect his wife. *I only want to know that she isn't suffering through a nightmare.*

His conscience said otherwise. Their dance last evening had only served to inflame his growing desire for his wife. He enjoyed having her close, the feel of her hand within his. He'd once dreamed of strolling through a meadow, hand in hand with the woman he loved. *Loved.* He gave up on that fantasy years ago.

Once he entered his room, he thought twice about going to her. No, he didn't *need* to see her. He would be back in London soon enough.

Sitting down in the large brown leather chair, he started to put his feet on the stool, then shot up and paced the length of the room. He paused for a moment, certain that he heard her cry out.

Silence.

Trudging his way to the window, he pondered their relationship. Faith had been the wife he'd thought he hadn't wanted. He still vowed to never fall in love, which would only lead to heartbreak. *I could protect her and make her happy without falling in love.* Most marriages of the *ton* had survived on far less.

He caught his reflection in the window. The black of the night absorbed his image. He turned away. Rubbing the back of his neck, he paced back and forth, unable to control the inferno spiraling inside. In one heartbeat, his mind was made up.

Damn, he swore to himself as he marched to her suite. Once he crossed the threshold to Faith's room, he knew there was no turning back.

He was expecting Faith to be asleep, but instead, she was sitting in bed sketching. A slender leg peeked from beneath the sensible white nightgown, and her smooth creamy skin begged for exploration. He wanted to kiss his way up…

Visibly startled by his appearance, she questioned, "Is anything the matter?"

Stamping down improper thoughts, he cleared his throat. "May I come in?" She nodded her head, and he approached the bed. "What are you drawing?"

She held one of the sketches out to him. "Just some of my favorite flowers. I couldn't sleep." She leaned forward and watched as he looked at her work. "What do you think?"

He was amazed at the detail she was able to achieve. "Quite impressive," he said as he took another sketch from the bed. He hadn't known she could draw. *And why would you, when you haven't taken the time to know her likes and interests?* He was going to change that.

Her eyes beamed at the compliment, and her cheeks blushed. "Do you think…? That is, would you mind…?"

He sat on the bed and placed a finger under her chin, prompting her to look at him. He adored her sweet shyness and he could deny her nothing in that moment. "What are you trying to say?"

The words rushed out, "May I redesign the orangery? I was thinking that if we took out some of the palms, we could incorporate—" She stopped mid-sentence, grabbed some pillows, and stacked them against the headboard. "Sit here and I'll show you the sketches I've been working on." Her hand brushed his shoulder as she adjusted the pillow. Much to his relief, she did not flinch or move away.

He had never been interested in Deer Park, had left most of the details to his steward, but her excitement was contagious. Not only did he find himself listening attentively, but also adding suggestions of his own. For the first time he could recall, he felt a sense of pride at being the Marquess of Hawthorne.

He was enjoying their evenings together. They talked about all manner of likes and interests. He had never shared this much of himself with anyone, not even his closest friends.

Faith put her head down on his chest and chattered away about her plans, not only for the orangery, but for the garden as well. He listened with half an ear, too tempted by his dainty wife to stay focused on herbs for long. His thoughts drifted to that first night he'd spent with her in this bed and every night since. He came to the realization that he had never spent so much time clothed in bed in his entire adult life.

Faith raised her head off his chest and looked into his eyes, her gaze never wavering. "Why did you marry me?" The question came out of nowhere.

His muscles tensed. "Your father demanded it, and here we are." He no longer suspected her an accomplice to the blackmail and did not want to discuss it further.

Clearly, his wife did not feel the same.

"You did not compromise me. You did nothing wrong. On the contrary, you saved me. Why did you feel obligated?" She licked her lips, waiting for him to answer.

Why was she questioning him about this now?

"The reason is not up for discussion." He did not want to argue, did not want to spoil the moment. There were still too many unanswered questions surrounding that evening, ones that might never be answered.

She came to a sitting position and brought her knees to her chin. She did not say a word, but stared at him with big blue eyes. She simply waited as the moments ticked by.

He could not stand it any longer. Her charming smile and endearing gaze would be his undoing. "He blackmailed me," he blurted out. "My cousin had got a young woman with child. Your father discovered the information and threatened to go to my grandmother with the news."

"But surely you could explain what…"

He shook his head. "I wanted to protect my grandmother from the gossiping tongues and could think of no way out of the predicament than…"

Faith turned from him. "Marrying me." Her words were a mere whisper, barely audible, but the hurt in her voice was loud and clear.

He leaned forward, cupped the nape of her neck, and stroked her cheek with his thumb, forcing her to look at him when she would have otherwise looked away.

Her eyes were bright with unshed tears. "I'm truly sorry you were forced to marry me." Her words tore at his heart.

"I'm not."

He wasn't sorry in the least. He wanted Faith as his wife. The declaration struck him like a bolt of lightning. He pressed a soft kiss to her lips. Her gasp was like the sun peeking through the clouds on a stormy day, full of hope and warmth.

"Marcus…" she whispered his name, and in that moment, he lost his heart forever.

·   ·   ·

"Marcus…" she sighed, but before she could finish her thought, he deepened the kiss. And what a glorious kiss it was.

Little by little, with each passing day, their relationship had grown into something more than two people forced together, pretending to have a happy marriage. Faith no longer feared Marcus or the unknown. She wanted to be near him, to share her secrets, to be held by him. Something had changed with their kiss. She couldn't possibly explain what, but she felt an intense desire to tell him her secret. She pulled back from him, her breathing heavy with a mixture of hunger and anxiety.

"I need to confess."

Pain streaked across his face, the spot between his brows crinkled in confusion.

Doubts rose from within. Perhaps she was wrong to want to tell him. It was too late now—she had already begun to dig her own grave. The knot that had begun in her stomach was traveling up her throat. She closed her eyes and begged her emotions to cooperate.

She opened her eyes to Marcus' hard stare. All words lodged in her throat. Hurt and betrayal distorted his features. What had he endured as a child? His words were slow and methodical. "What have you done?"

"I've never lied to you," she blurted out, wanting to ease his doubts. "I need to tell you… about my… childhood." Not the happy stories they had already shared. She needed to tell him the ugly things, so he would understand.

His features softened by slow measures, and his breathing evened, but he remained silent.

She did not know where to begin. Apart from her lady's maid, she had never told anyone before, had kept everything bottled inside where it had gradually eaten away at whatever happiness she'd tried to hold on to.

"When my mother was alive, my father was… different." She took a deep breath and exhaled slowly. "But when Mama…" Painful memories of that distant day when her mother died flashed before her. She could not speak those words. "My sister raised me, protected me. But when she…" Screams in the night echoed through her ears, and she could not stop the tears from streaming down her cheeks. "He beat her, too." The words left her mouth on a hiccup, in barely a whisper, but she knew Marcus had heard them.

He took her hand. His question held none of the disgust she feared. "Can you tell me what happened?"

She nodded and then, on a long slow breath, pushed the words past her lips, "After Mary died, it was only the two of us." The words felt strangled in her throat, but she had to speak them. Faith took several deep breaths before continuing. "Father was gone for long periods of time, and when he returned home, he always seemed happy. But then his mood would darken, and he would start to drink. He blamed me for looking like my mother, and that is what started it. I tried to be a good girl, but he never believed me, always accusing me of scandalous behavior. Whenever he drank, I would run away and hide."

He reached out to her, held her. "I will never let him hurt you again." His gentle kindness was her undoing. She collapsed onto his chest, his white shirt soaking up the tears.

"I'm sorry." She continued to sob. "I wanted to tell you, but…"

"Shh, it's all right. I'm sorry for losing my temper." He kissed the top of her head. "I will never let him hurt you again," he repeated in a shaky breath.

Not for the first time, she wondered what had happened in his youth. But she didn't want to ponder that at the moment. There were other things she desired.

Marcus had never demanded his husbandly rights, had

never taken what she did not offer. She'd been too frightened to speak, to take that next step. She knew that, at some point, she would have to resign herself to becoming his wife in full. The thought had always scared her, until tonight.

Now she wanted to be his wife, and not only in name. She couldn't explain it, but there was an almost desperate need to be close to him, to feel him, to be consumed by him. Her fingers ached with a trembling desire to touch, explore. With her forefinger, she traced the outline of his firm jaw. He watched her every move, his eyes darkened to a rich golden brown, but he did not say a word.

She leaned in and kissed his lips. Their breath intermingled, sending warmth that filled her body from head to toe. The room grew hotter with each breath she took.

Marcus' fingers circled up her arm, across her shoulder, resting at the base of her neck. Her skin tingled and came to life with each new touch. The fluttering in her heart was not from fear, but from something else entirely unfamiliar, but the prospect was all too enticing.

He began to unbutton the column of small pearls that started at the delicate spot at the base of her throat and continued down to where her heart beat wildly in her chest. His ministrations were slow and methodical. Her body screamed with want and need, while her chest rose and fell with the undoing of each button.

He pulled her nightgown over her head and tossed it to one side. She saw his features tighten, his eyes flash with anger for a split second. The breath caught in her throat.

That scar.

A hideous, jagged red line, which started at the top of her right shoulder and snaked its way for several inches down her arm. It was a constant reminder of her father's drunken rages.

She edged away, her stomach tightening.

"Please don't pull away." His words were soft and caring. There was no hint of pity or disgust in his tone or manner. He kissed her shoulder where the scar began. "I want to take away your pain, give you pleasure."

His promise warmed her heart and filled her with joy. She felt safe with him. Her husband might have a temper at times, but she knew without a doubt that he would never harm her, that something in his youth was the source of those dark moods.

She tried to unbutton his shirt, but her hands would not cooperate. She'd only managed to undo two buttons when he took her hands in his and kissed each palm.

"Let me help you." His voice was deep and husky. He gave her a seductive half-smile that made her insides somersault.

No sooner had he started the task than he was finished. She had never thought anyone could undress with such speed. He rejoined her on the bed and pulled her into him. His body was large and strong, but she did not fear him.

He lowered his head to hers, their breath intermingling, sending a warm shiver down her body. What began as a simple kiss deepened as his tongue explored her mouth, his hand running up her inner thigh, caressing, delving. She had never known her body was capable of feeling such pleasure. She wanted more... so much more.

Muscles rippled beneath her roaming fingers. She could not escape the heat of his skin as every inch of her body screamed with want.

"Faith," his breath was gravelly in her ear, "I don't want to hurt you."

She saw the anguish in his eyes. Taking his cheeks in her hands, she kissed away his doubts. "I know I am safe with you."

Her husband took his time loving her, bringing her pleasure in ways she never thought possible. His touch was gentle, caring, and she gave herself without reserve.

In the aftermath of their lovemaking, she nuzzled into him, his calm, even breathing inducing her own sleep. She hoped she wouldn't wake in the morning to find this had all been a beautiful dream.

CHAPTER 8

*M*arcus had not seen his wife since earlier that morning, and damn it, he missed her. He had never imagined that his life could be this complete. He'd often envied such happiness in other couples, but never dared to hope that one woman could wipe away the pain from his childhood. All seemed right with his world.

He had spent the morning arranging for a special surprise for Faith. Thomas had been able to acquire additional holly, ivy, evergreens, and even some mistletoe. With her lady's maid's assistance, he decorated Faith's room while she was toiling away in the orangery.

Swags of ivy intertwined with blue ribbon were wound around each post of the bed. Garlands of evergreens were draped from the mantel. He took special care to hang mistletoe sporadically through the room and especially over the bed.

He stood back and admired their work. The crisp smell of winter greenery wafted through the air on the heels of clove, reminding him of that first night when he'd come home to Deer Park. The room was ready. Now all he needed was his wife. He couldn't wait to surprise her. She had brought the meaning of Christmastide back into his heart.

He was still not fond of the orangery—he didn't think he could ever escape the pain it evoked—but at least he didn't dread coming here now. There were no evil spirits lurking anymore to destroy his happiness—quite the opposite.

The day was pleasant, the sun was bright, and there was not a cloud in the sky. The short walk to the orangery helped to clear his mind. Artemisia and Nigel had decided to take advantage of the amiable weather. With Mat in tow, they'd agreed on a picnic. He would have Faith all to himself for a couple more hours. There was much he wanted to say to her.

Through the hazy glass, he could see the silhouette of two ladies. The first was definitely that of his wife's. He had come to know her petite figure and glorious shimmering blonde hair. Reflections of the intimacy they shared last night set his pulse aflame.

The second outline looked to be that of Aunt Lou, although he had thought she was in her room resting. Shaking off the thought, he opened the glass door. The sweet scent of newly bloomed lilacs swirled about him, reminding him of...

"Mother?" His body stilled. His *mother* was standing next to his *wife*. For a brief moment, he felt the life drain from him.

The older woman's head whipped around. He wasn't imagining her. She was just as he remembered, only older. Hazel eyes met his. She looked like a fox cornered by the hounds.

"Marcus," she choked on his name.

The last time he had seen her was in this very place twenty-five years ago.

Lies, all lies.

He backed away, oblivious to all sounds around him.

"Stop lying to me!" His voice ricocheted through the space as demons from the past threatened to consume him.

His mother approached with tears in her eyes, but her words would not fool him again. "I had no choice. He threatened to harm you."

FAITH WATCHED the scene unfold with a helplessness she had not felt in years. Images of a dark night stormed her mind.

"You've decided to marry? Who gave you the right to decide?"

"But, Papa, I love him."

"What about me and your sister?"

"Faith could come to live with us."

"I will not allow you to leave, or take Faith away from me."

A loud crack rang through her mind, bringing her back into the present. Holding her hand to her temple, Faith tried to focus.

Where was Marcus?

"This is what I had always feared," Mrs. Gardner cried. "And now I have lost him forever."

Blinking away the remnants of past unpleasantness, Faith returned to the present, and the shocking news that just unfolded.

Marcus' mother was alive!

Disbelief weighed her thoughts. She approached the woman she'd only known as Mrs. Gardner until a few moments ago, too many questions storming her mind all at once.

"You're probably wondering why I pretended to be dead all these years?" the older woman said with such sadness in her eyes.

That was one of many questions on Faith's mind. "Yes."

The two women talked for nearly an hour, offering each other comfort. Faith could not fault Marcus' mother for her action or precautions she took. Over the past months, she had grown to love this lady. After living with her father, Faith understood why Marcus' mother had felt she should leave all those years ago. She would have suffocated and died because the abuse meted out by her late husband. She'd left not only for her own well-being but that of her son as well.

She brought her mother-in-law into a warm embrace. "You have to give your son time. He will forgive you, but first you must talk to him, tell him all that you told me."

"I wish I shared your optimism."

HOT, molten anger burned his throat. Marcus grabbed the bottle and poured another three fingers of brandy. Swirling the amber liquid, he wondered where he had gone wrong. This morning had seemed so bright and full of possibilities, and now his world was turned upside down. The mother he thought was dead had been very much alive. She hadn't died. She had deserted him.

Could this day get any worse?

The ache in his heart swelled to epic proportions. He gulped the liquid in one swallow. The burning spirit settled in the pit of his stomach next to guilt and anxiety. He was about to pour another glass when the door to his study swung open wide, thudding against the wall.

"My lord…" Caspar began, but was abruptly cut off.

"No need to announce me." He heard his grandmother's gruff voice before he saw her plump figure push past Caspar. "Where is she?"

Marcus stood speechless. What was his grandmother doing here? And which "she" was the matriarch referring to? The woman he'd been forced to marry, or his recently returned-from-the-dead mother?

His head pounded like the rumble of thunder storming across an angry dark night. Life had been much simpler when he was a rake about town and his greatest worry was avoiding starry-eyed debutants.

He was about to ask for clarification when both his wife *and* his mother entered the room. His mama stopped at the threshold, all color drained from her face. "Miriam."

"Natalie." The tone of Marcus' grandmother's voice was rough, harsh, but she didn't seem surprised that his mother was alive.

"So, my informant was correct. I thought I told you never to come here again," his grandmother scolded.

"*You* told my mother never—" he began.

Grandmother did not allow him to finish his sentence as she turned a suspicious eye to Faith. "And who are you?"

He would have to get answers to *his* questions later. Sucking in a deep breath, he steeled himself for the dramatics that were about to commence. "Grandmother, allow me to introduce my wife, Lady Hawthorne."

"Your wife?" His grandmother's voice raised an octave. "When did this happen? Why was my approval not sought?"

"I did not need your approval to marry." He would not give his grandmother any cud to chew. He'd keep to the story he'd originally told his aunt. "It was love at first sight, and I have no regrets." He could not escape noticing the grimace on the elderly woman's face before it turned to a look of pure hatred.

"No regrets? You have thrown everything away on some… some tart!"

"You will not speak of my wife in such a manner," Marcus growled. "She—"

"You have ruined everything that I have worked so hard to achieve for this family." Grandmother pointed a long, boney finger at him. "Everything I have done has been for your benefit."

That was the last straw. Every muscle in his body tensed, his fists tightened, and his short nails dug into his palms.

"My benefit? You told me my mother was dead. Even after Father died, you continued with the pretense. How was that to my benefit?" His voice reverberated through the room, his temper rising with each breath he took.

"She had a lover and would have brought scandal to this family." Grandmother's response was one of nonchalance intertwined with justification.

"I never had a lover!" Mother cried. "You and your horrible son made that up." She turned toward Marcus and implored, "You must believe me. I did not want to go away, but I couldn't stay."

Marcus stared down into his mother's eyes, that were so much like his own. She never flinched or looked away, but held his gaze. "Why couldn't you stay?" He needed to know. No matter how disturbing it was to hear, he needed to know the truth.

She closed her eyes and took in a deep breath, but still she did not speak.

Faith walked up behind her and stroked her arm. "Tell him," she whispered softly into her ear.

Opening her eyes, Mother looked him directly in the eyes. She swallowed hard. "Your father beat me."

Marcus did not know what he expected to hear, but learning of his father's cruelty toward her turned his stomach. The truth was worse than he had imagined.

"It's a lie!" His grandmother insisted. "My Talbot would never harm a woman who didn't deserve it."

Marcus turned a harsh gaze on his grandmother. "And did Father believe my mother deserved it?"

With each second that ticked by, his grandmother became more agitated. She blinked in rapid succession before the words spewed from her mouth. "Of course, she deserved it. She was not obedient. Not loving in the ways a wife should be. He was only trying to mold her into the perfect marchioness."

Why?

None of it made sense to Marcus. Why would his father treat his mother so? He looked into his grandmother's muted brown eyes. "Was it because Mother was *only* the daughter of a baronet?" Images of his father drinking heavily and mumbling in a drunken stupor fought their way through the haze of suppressed memories. "Or was it because Father had higher aspirations within the *ton*?" Realization dawned. "Mother was never good enough for Father. Was it because of prestige, money, or something more nefarious?" He wanted answers.

"No, my Talbot was the most honest of men." Grandmother's declaration did not sit well with Marcus. "We needed to ensure the title stayed close at hand. We needed a spare, but your mother continually refused my poor Talbot. What were we supposed to do?"

"So, you decided to rid her from my life so that Father could have a chance to sire a spare?"

It was beginning to make more sense. Not long after his father had emerged from mourning, he—along with half the eligible male population—had begun courting Lady Barbara. Not only was she the daughter of a well-connected duke, but she was exceptionally beautiful, accomplished, wealthy, and one of the most sought-after women of the *ton*.

Lady Barbara could have had her pick of gentlemen and chose the firstborn son of a duke, solidifying her position within society.

Marcus did not understand why at the time, but his father became very angry after being shunned, retreating from polite society, and hiding behind heavy spirits and loose women.

Still not believing the web of excuses that Grandmother wove, he decided to play devil's advocate. "He didn't need a spare. There were plenty of cousins."

"Distant cousins. I was not going to allow any of Jeremy's boys to inherit." Grandmother's voice was firm, unwavering. She stood with her shoulders back, her eyes narrowed on him, daring him to challenge her further.

"What gave you the right to destroy people's happiness? Through the years I have tried to protect you, protect this family, from scandal. I thought my mother abandoned me for her lover and then died. I thought my father was the victim. But it was all a lie. My entire existence has been a lie. I want you gone from this house before the day is out." He heard his grandmother's sharp intake of breath, but would not appease her. Not this time. Not ever again.

Faith walked around Mother so that she was only a couple of feet away from him, but it might as well have been on the other side of the world, the distance between them was so great. He did not need her sympathy.

He was upset and confused about everything that had transpired. He did not know what he felt. Betrayal, anger, confusion, happiness, and guilt all struggled for his attention. It was too much to absorb.

He extended his hand to stop Faith. He could not even think of two coherent words to put together. He shook his head and stomped out of the room.

CHAPTER 9

$\mathcal{I}$t was late, or rather, very early, as Marcus approached Deer Park from the west and watched the sun rise over the slumbering land. The aura of Christmastide had dimmed beneath the realization that his entire life was a fabrication. He had stayed away all night, riding, trying to clear his mind. He was exhausted, Ameriko was exhausted, but still he found no relief.

Every truth he had grown up with had been a lie. Aunt Lou was the one exception. And she was only his aunt through marriage to his father's brother. But not even her kind words had diminished the sourness churning in his stomach.

In the distance, Deer Park looked so peaceful in the early morning light. Anyone seeing it now would never suspect the troubles that lurked within its walls. Despite everything, one thing was for certain; he was no longer a frightened, unsure child, but a grown man with responsibilities, and it was time to face his demons once and for all.

He did not go to his room, or to Faith's, for that matter. His head was still cloudy with everything that had been revealed and he'd experienced over the last week. He just needed some time to clear his head.

Slipping into his study unnoticed, he breathed a sigh of relief.

"Where have you been? I've been waiting for you." His mother's anxious voice came from a dark corner of the room.

"I'm a grown man." He walked across the elegant carpet to the windows and pulled the heavy drapes aside, revealing the awakening landscape. Soft rays of light streamed into the muted space.

"A mother never stops worrying." He heard the concern in her voice, but chose to ignore it.

Keeping his back toward her, he questioned, "Is that what this is? Concern? Why, after all these years…"

"I was afraid. I was afraid of exactly what happened. Your grandmother has always controlled this family. I was relieved when I learned you went to live with Lou. She is a good woman."

That was one point they could both agree on.

"Why are you here?" He wanted answers, not concoctions and false pretenses.

"You left in such a fury and when you did not return… I was worried about you."

"I didn't mean here in this study." His patience was hanging by a thread. "Why did you come back?"

His mother walked to where he was standing. The sweet scent of lilac wrapped about him. "I never left."

For the second time in less than twenty-four hours, Marcus' world had tipped on its side. *Was this some sort of cruel joke?* He held his breath, waiting for her to explain.

"Even after your father threatened me to stay away, I couldn't. I had to see you, to know that you were safe. I wanted to watch you grow up. Your father rarely spent time in the country, so I could move about without attracting notice."

Pointing out the obvious, Marcus stated, "But there are servants everywhere."

She shook her head. "Caspar knew everything. He made certain I could always see you, even if only from a distance."

Marcus was going to have to have a word with *his* butler. First his dog, now his butler, was no one loyal to him?

"After your father died, I was so desperate to see you that I went to your grandmother, but she continued to refuse me. Her threats were just as strong as your father's." The layer of betrayal that had haunted him since he was a child began to disappear. Mother *had* wanted him.

He needed to know everything—no more secrets, no more lies. He needed the truth, all of it. "I want to know what he did to you. Everything."

They talked for hours, both making amends for past wrongs. He was glad his mother was alive. It had been a difficult journey, but somehow his path seemed straighter, less inhibited. He knew the future *would* be brighter.

Before his mother took her leave, she offered her wisdom. "Although Faith never revealed how the two of you came to be husband and wife, I suspect it was not the usual path to the altar." There was a long pause. She came up to him and put her hand on his arm. "Go and talk to her. She loves you so much."

Marcus stood motionless, too stunned to speak. *Faith loved him?* What had he done to earn such a reward? In the past couple of days, things *had* changed between them, but she loved him?

Whenever she was near, his world was better, but he did not want love. Truth be told, he was afraid of losing it. No, he was perfectly content with keeping Faith safe and avoiding all emotional entanglement.

Liar.

Hours' worth of estate business, or rather, issues, had kept Marcus sequestered in his study. He had just finished the last of it when a firm knock sounded on the door.

"There is a Mr. Johnson here to see you, my lord," Caspar said with disdain. Clearly, this Mr. Johnson was not a tenant in need.

Crossing his arms, Marcus questioned, "Did he say what it is in regard to?"

"He said it was urgent, and he was only at liberty to discuss the matter with you."

Marcus did not have the tolerance to deal with this. There were too many emotions he was still sorting through, not to mention that he still had not worked up the courage to speak with Faith.

Shaking his head, he sighed, "Send him in."

Within a matter of moments, Caspar ushered in a young man who looked no more than twenty. His appearance was clean, but his clothing was simple and outdated.

He fumbled with the hat in his hands, clearly nervous about this meeting. There was something familiar about him, but Marcus could not place his finger on it.

"Thank you for seeing me, Lord Hawthorne. My name is Johnson." Marcus did not recall ever meeting a Mr. Johnson. "I came to confess."

Another confession?

Why did everyone all of a sudden feel the need to own up and disrupt his life? This was supposed to be a joyous time of year.

He was expecting the young man to reveal he'd stolen

from his land or something of the sort. "Proceed." He could not hide the impatient tone from his voice.

The young lad gulped hard. "Mr. Whitworth promised to pay me lots of money if I did it. I didn't want to, but my ma was sick and my da is dead, and my younger brothers and sisters would have starved." Wringing his tattered brown hat, he added, "I didn't want to do it, but I needed the money."

Heat rose and Marcus' blood began to boil. "What did Whitworth ask you to do?" He suspected the answer, but needed to know for certain.

"He… he asked me to…" The young lad bobbed his head this way and that. "He said that you compromised his daughter and then refused to marry her, and that it was the only way to get you to do what was right."

Marcus did not rejoice in knowing his suspicions were correct. What kind of father would arrange for his daughter to be treated in such a manner? She was a victim in more ways than one.

Gritting his teeth, he attempted to maintain his composure, at least until he had his answers. "Why did you come here and tell me all this now?"

Johnson hung his head low. "Mr. Whitworth came to me and said he had another job."

Marcus was going to kill Whitworth. His voice rumbled, "Bloody hell, boy, what…" He stopped his rant mid-sentence and took in a deep breath to steady his raging pulse. He was trying to be patient, trying not to lose his temper with this young man who was trying to do the right thing. He needed to glean information from him, and losing his temper was not going to achieve that end. "What sort of job?"

"He asked me to help him kidnap…" The lad's words trailed off and the pained expression on his face said it all. "I told him no, and he got so angry…." He gulped hard. "I don't want harm to come to her."

Images of Faith flashed before him. Marcus had come to care for his wife in more ways than he could even comprehend at the moment. He did not want to lose her. He could *not* lose her.

Time was of the essence.

"Casper!" Marcus bellowed. His faultless butler was in the room in two strides. "Where's my wife?"

"In the orangery with Lady Hawthorne."

Marcus did not waste a single moment. Dread settling in his stomach, he stormed through the house, ignoring anyone who crossed his path. Sounds and voices eddied around him.

The quickest path to the orangery was through the kitchen and down the short, winding path. He took no notice of the world around him. Once clear of the house, he picked up his pace and ran with every bit of energy he could muster. Balder barking insistently in the distance only added to the sinking feeling in the pit of his stomach, which grew worse with each stride. His breath puffed white clouds in the cold afternoon air.

He was a step away from the orangery entrance when he heard a blood-curdling cry through the glass.

CHAPTER 10

Faith heard the door to the orangery open and close. Not looking up from the topiary she had yet to perfect, she called out, "Good afternoon, Mat," assuming it was Mathilda coming to visit again. The little girl had expressed her boredom earlier with everyone else preoccupied with tomorrow's early departure to Knollwood for the remainder of the yuletide festivities.

"Good afternoon, my darling daughter." The sound of her father's voice sent a chill down her spine, his condescending tone turning her blood cold.

Faith and Marcus' mother turned around in unison. Faith hardly recognized her father. His unshaven face and disheveled appearance were so uncharacteristic of him. Only the odd twitch in his eye was familiar. It told her he was up to no good.

The heat rose in her cheeks, her knees started to shake, and tremors engulfed her entire being. But before she could succumb to those sensations, a petite hand gave her own hand a firm squeeze. She was not alone. Somehow, that gave her the courage to speak.

"What are you doing here?"

"What kind of welcome is that for your father?" The older man looked around him. "You've done quite well for yourself."

With each step he took forward, Faith and Lady Hawthorne retreated. The back of Faith's legs met with the grey stone bench. It had been one of her favorite spots, but now it lost its luster.

Her father tsked several times before continuing with a deep cackle. "How unfortunate that you won't be able to continue to enjoy it, you ungrateful wench."

Too paralyzed with fear, Faith could not find the words to answer him. Her father continued to come closer and closer. Cornered, there was nowhere for them to run, but Lady Hawthorne never let go of her hand.

Marcus' mother stood tall and raised her chin. "You had best leave now; my son is due to arrive at any moment. He will not be pleased to see you." Even though her words were firm, her hand trembled within Faith's.

Faith's father paid no heed to the older woman's threat. His gaze was centered on her. "I sacrificed my life so that you could be married to a titled lord, and you repay me by barring me entrance, refusing to share all that the *ton* has to offer. What would your poor mother say to that, and what about your sister who sacrificed her own life to keep you safe?"

Images of Mary flashed in rapid succession across Faith's mind. She closed her eyes to keep her head from spinning. Mary, clinging to the last threads of life, gasping for air, trying to tell her something, came to the forefront. *Be a good girl and do as he says.*

She opened her eyes and met her father's cruel gaze. "You monster." Her voice was calm and even. Once she started, the words kept flowing. "You killed Mary, and you would have killed me too if I'd stayed."

Lady Hawthorne kept a tight hold on Faith's hand, encouraging her to speak, to rid herself of the fear and demons that had ruled her life for so long. Words that she'd never dared to say to her father before.

"You hurt me, but I never ran. I let you say horrible things to me and never defended myself. I let you manipulate me." Faith paused, mustering her courage. "Never again."

"What I did was for your own good, but you never appreciated anything." The desperate edge to her father's voice did nothing to lessen her resolve. She stood her ground even as he continued to chastise her. "I am right, you are wrong. I am older than you, and I know better." In one long stride, he closed the distance between them. "You need to learn your place."

Before she could register what was happening, he clasped a firm hand about her neck. She gulped for air, fighting to keep her wits about her.

No, I won't let you win.

Lady Hawthorne tugged on Whitworth's arm, fighting to release his grip. Faith's world started to darken as little gasps of air exited her mouth. Mustering what little strength she had, she fought through the pain and haze and tried to kick him. Her skirt twisted about her legs as she struggled. Her strength to fight was waning.

"Let her go," Lady Hawthorne demanded shrilly, tugging on his arm. The motion only caused Whitworth's grip to tighten more. Faith could feel the breath leaving her lungs with painful rasps. "Let her…"

His hand was suddenly gone. Unable to control her balance, Faith collapsed to the floor, clutching her chest, gasping for air.

Out of the corner of her eye, she saw Lady Hawthorne

pounding her fist on her father's chest. Their words were slow to reach her ears. She watched the scene unfolding as if she weren't in her own body. Lady Hawthorne continued to kick and fight, but her father was much stronger.

Faith watched with horror as her father grabbed hold of Lady Hawthorne and flung her to one side, the woman's head making contact with the cold stone bench.

"Nooo!" The strangled cry left Faith's lips and vibrated through the vast space. She tried to scramble to where Lady Hawthorne lay motionless, but her father was already upon her, dragging her across the flagstone floor. The edge of her skirt caught on an ornamental rock, stopping their progress. She tried to speak, but her father's harsh hand slapped across her face and silenced any words that might have been forthcoming.

She swung her arm, but he caught her wrist and squeezed. "Do not even think of trying to fight me," he growled at her. With one hand firmly gripping her, he brought the other down hard on her back. Jolts of air caught in her throat.

She retreated inward, trying to numb herself. *It will be over soon*, she chanted in her mind. *Soon...*

A loud crash from beyond rattled her senses. Commotion rang out from all directions.

One moment her father was standing over her, the next, Marcus was pummeling him.

Relief coursed through her body, easing her breathing. *Marcus had come for her.*

Ignoring the pain that was exploding through every inch of her body, she crawled over to Lady Hawthorne's limp body.

"Please hang on… please don't die."

. . .

MARCUS RAN and plowed headfirst into Whitworth's gut, sending the older man to the ground, then rolled on top of him, pulled him up by the collar, and punched him in the jaw. Pain coursed through his knuckles with continued contact, but he did not care. Years of pent-up rage surfaced. Every ounce of anger and frustration, every insult from his father, every betrayal, every lie was manifested into his punches.

Oblivious to everything around him, Marcus continued to pummel his quarry until the last thread of anger dissipated. Whitworth lay unconscious, but still breathing. Marcus would have killed the man if not for the presence of his wife.

His wife.

For the first time since entering the orangery, he took notice of his surroundings. Nigel and half of the staff had charged into the place. Aunt Lou was dictating orders at a rapid speed. Artemisia was inspecting his mother, whose skin was already blotched black and blue from Whitworth's onslaught. Faith was huddled next to Balder, who stood protectively at her side.

Marcus rushed over to his wife and dog. His hands were all over Faith, inspecting her face and neck.

"I'm fine," she murmured. "She tried to help me." She choked on the words as tears filled her eyes.

All breath escaped him when he saw a thin trickle of blood stream from his mother's forehead. He was just finding his way to her again, and now he feared he was about to lose her. There were so many lost years to make up for. *Please let her live.*

Artemisia eased his worst suspicions. "She's alive, but took a nasty cut to the head. I'll tend to her wounds. Try not to worry too much."

Marcus felt his lungs fill with air. He let out a long sigh. Everyone he cared most about was safe. He turned his attention back to Faith, scooped her up into his arms, and carried her away from this scene. She nuzzled her head into his shoulder, but did not say a word.

As they neared the entrance to the house, a flurry of activity whirled about them. Marcus moved through the chaos in a daze, holding his delicate wife in his arms. He carried her up the front steps and into the hall.

Caspar was giving orders for hot water to be brought up to the marchioness' suite, and Troth was yelling to Thomas to fetch her satchel of ointments.

Every candle in sight had been lit. The lingering scent of Christmastide filled the house, reminding him that this was supposed to be a joyous time. In a bizarre sort of way, he supposed it was.

By the time he had reached their rooms, the fire had been lit, towels had been laid out, a pitcher of hot water had been delivered, and Troth had set up her ointments.

"Set her down here, my lord." Troth moved the pillow under Faith's head.

In a tone that brooked no argument, Marcus made his will known. "I will tend to my wife's needs. Go and assist with my mother." Out of the corner of his eye, he saw Troth leave the room. Faith continued to look at him, but did not say a word.

He'd failed her.

"Can you ever forgive me for not arriving sooner, for not protecting you?" His voice cracked with restrained emotion.

He should have killed Whitworth for all the pain he'd caused her. He did not know what he would have done if he'd lost Faith. In a flash of a second, he realized what this unwanted wife had come to mean to him.

Her words were strained, hoarse. "You did protect me."

"But I wasn't there when he..."

She shook her head. Cupping his cheek in her palm, she

brought his head closer to hers, forcing him to look into her crystal blue eyes. "You saved me in more ways than you could possibly ever know. Thank you for rescuing me."

Her words made his heart swell with love, almost to the point of aching. "It was my pleasure."

EPILOGUE

K<nollwood Estate, Twelfth Night>

Everyone he cared about was at Knollwood. Even his convalescing mother insisted on making the journey. But the evening had been tiresome with all the guests gathered for the Twelfth Night festivities. Even though Faith was near throughout the evening, he still had to share her with the other guests. His patience was at an end.

Marcus had stared at the clock on the mantel for the past hour, waiting for the designated time to sneak Faith out of the great hall. He had wanted everything to be perfect. He wanted her all to himself.

"What if someone sees us?"

"Everyone is still enjoying the party." Kissing the tip of her nose, he whispered, "Come on." He tugged her hand, slipping behind a large tapestry.

"Where are we going?"

"You'll see in a moment." He hoped his orders had been

carried out precisely. All sounds died to a dull hum as they proceeded down the dark passageway. He had traversed this way many times throughout his youth and could find his way to the center courtyard blindfolded.

"I can't see anything," Faith giggled. How he adored that sweet sound. The hammering in his heart grew louder with each step.

When they reached the end of the secret passage, he took off Faith's gloves. "You won't be needing these." Actually, he wanted to take off much more than just her gloves, but there would be plenty of time for that later.

"What...?" He silenced her question with a deep kiss, savoring the taste of sugar cake on her lips.

"Close your eyes." He knew without even seeing her expression that she gave him a skeptical look.

"But it's already dark. Why do I—"

He brushed another kiss across her lips, silencing her protest. "Keep them closed and don't peek," he teased.

"Only if you tell me what this is all about."

"I have a surprise for you." As he opened the door leading to the courtyard, cool night air breezed past them. "Open your eyes."

The center courtyard was aglow with bright torches. The Great Oak stood proudly. Boughs of mistletoe with pearly white beads gleamed in the firelight.

"Where are we?" she said with astonishment.

"In the central courtyard." He guided her to one of the low-hanging branches dripping with mistletoe. "Legend has it that the first Lady Hawthorne—brought here as a bride—watered the Great Oak with her tears when her husband went off to war. Upon his safe return, a special celebration was held. That night a thunderstorm shook the land and lightning struck the tree with extraordinary force." Marcus pointed midway up the large trunk. "When dawn approached, everyone could see that their initials had been burned into the bark by the lightning. It was foretold that the two lovers would live a long and prosperous life together."

He had often glared at the markings of love engraved on the Great Oak with envy. Tonight was different.

"That is a beautiful story." Faith smiled as she gazed up through the branches at the dozens of initials that graced the old tree.

He had never been so nervous in his life. The pounding in his chest was almost too much to bear. What if she did not feel the same?

Taking her hands in his, he began, "Our marriage may not have started auspiciously, but you have brightened my life and proved that true love does exist. You have shown me that despite my faults and temper, I am worthy of love... your love."

"Oh, Marcus," she sighed as she brought his hand to her lips and pressed a delicate kiss against it.

Keeping her hands in his, he kneeled down on one knee. "Lady Hawthorne, will you do me the honor of accepting my hand in marriage?"

A giggle sprung from her lips.

His heart plummeted. This was not the response he was hoping for.

"But we're already married," she said, with confused amusement.

He stood and guided her closer to one of the low-hanging branches. "Yes, but the first time, I didn't ask. I want to do this correctly. I have made far too many mistakes in my life. I don't want to ever lose you."

Her features softened, and her lovely blue eyes filled with loving tenderness. "You won't—"

He silenced her words with a gentle kiss, relishing in the feel of her soft lips. A moment later, he pulled back and rested his forehead against hers. "I have something for you," he whispered as he brushed a kiss on her cheek.

Pulling his great-grandmother's wedding ring from his pocket, he placed it on her delicate finger. Eight little pearls that glistened like the white berries on the mistletoe, reminding him of their first kiss, surrounded the rose-cut diamond.

"I love you. I think I loved you from the moment we first met." The words flowed from his mouth as if they were the most natural words in the English language to say.

Faith's mouth curved with a tenderness he found most endearing. She stood on her tiptoes, wrapped her arms around his neck, and pressed her dainty figure firmly against his. "Oh Marcus, I love you, too," she whispered against his lips.

For the first time in his life, Marcus believed in the legend of the Great Oak.

Want to know what happens next? Keep reading for a
chapter excerpt from
Dancing Around the Truth
Book Four in *A Waltz with Destiny* Series…

Chapter One excerpt from
Dancing Around the Truth

SPRING, *1822*

"You won't agree to a season, you won't attend any country dances, and you won't even go to a house party. Damn it, Isabel, I am at my wits' end with you." Weston ran a frustrated hand through his hair, practically pulling it out by the roots. His sister was perhaps the most stubborn creature ever to walk the earth.

"Don't you use such language with me." Isabel wagged a delicate finger at him. "Just because you're miserable does not mean you have to make the rest of us miserable, too."

Pressing his fingers to his temple, Weston tried to rub the pain away, but the source of it was still in the room. He did not think he could endure another of his sister's lectures on what was wrong with his life. "I swear, one of these days I am going to tie you up and toss you on your uncle's doorstep."

"You wouldn't," Isabel walked up to him and jabbed her finger into his chest. "You know very well that Father wanted me under your care, and besides, such tactics would not work. As soon as I was able, I would return here." She ended her declaration with a smug smile.

"It really is a lost cause," Isabel's companion, Anastasia, chimed in.

Weston glared at her, wishing Anastasia would not take sides. He'd promised his late father that he would ensure Isabel had at least one season. Four years later, and he still had not managed to fulfill that promise. At the very least, he wanted his bluestocking of a sister to be open to the idea. He was about to argue as much when Milton entered the study, salver in hand.

Weston took the card from the tray. He sucked in a deep breath and mentally groaned. *Damn.* "See her into the drawing room."

"Yes, sir." Weston waited for Milton to leave before addressing his sister. It was common knowledge that servants talked, but he did not need to give them additional fodder.

"This isn't over, Isabel." She began to shake her head, but

he gave her no opportunity to protest. "We *will* discuss this later. You *will* honor Father's wishes."

Isabel gave him her classic "that's what you think" look and then stormed from the room.

Anastasia started to follow Isabel, but then stopped in front of him. "Perhaps a different approach would be better next time. Possibly a bribe of some sort." Every conversation he ever had with his sister ended the same way. He was curious to hear more about the new approach Anastasia suggested, but the untimely arrival of Mrs. Keates interfered with that inquiry.

Several minutes later, he found himself outside the drawing room, preparing to do battle with yet another stubborn woman. Only this one had no idea what his involvement in her life was.

He entered and was instantly assaulted by an intoxicating mixture of lavender and vanilla. Philippa had only been there five minutes and already the room smelled like her. *Damn.* Best to get this over with as soon as possible.

"Good afternoon, Mrs. Keates." He hated that name. He hated even more that she had been married to a blackguard. At least she was free of him now. Her widow's weeds were a reminder of that.

"Just because I am here on official investigative business doesn't mean you have to be so formal with me. Really, Weston, we have known each other for a score of years or more."

Formality had always helped keep feelings at bay. He would be damned. "To what do I owe this visit, *Philippa?*"

"That's better. I came as soon as Aunt Imogene was settled." Philippa opened her black reticule, looking for something as she continued to speak. "The journey up from London was quite exhausting for her. But she informed me that, at her age, life in general is exhausting."

Weston could not possibly guess what was so dire that she would feel the need to travel here from London and not just send word. "You must be tired as well after the journey. Shall I ring for tea?"

Philippa looked at him, her crystal blue eyes holding a sadness that broke his heart. "No, no, I want to... that is..." She worried her bottom lip and pulled two letters from her reticule and handed them to him. "I guess I should start with these. Father asked that I deliver them to you."

He scanned the contents of the first letter, which was from Philippa's father, asking him to investigate the second letter. Unfolding it, he carefully read the demand for payment. After the death of his son-in-law six months previous, Lord Germayne had asked Weston to make enquiries into all of Alfred Keates' finances and activities. It had taken several months, and Weston had believed that he had uncovered all of Mr. Keates' unsavory dealings and cancelled his debts, but alas, apparently there was still some outstanding.

"I will write to your father and tell him that I will look into the matter."

He was about to excuse himself so that he could return to dealing with his unreasonable relation when Philippa spoke up. "There's more."

What more could there be? The blackguard Keates had accumulated more than five thousand pounds' worth of debt in the two years he and Philippa had been married. That was in addition to squandering her substantial dowry.

Philippa looked about the room. The seconds drew out, then when she finally spoke, her words were delivered in a hushed tone as if trying to keep the walls from hearing. "A Mrs. Keates visited me while I was in London."

Weston attempted to add shock to his voice without giving anything away. "Your late husband's mother visited you?"

"No, not his mother, but a woman claiming to be Alfred's wife."

Weston did not want to raise suspicion, and instead tried to brush the matter off. "Surely you must be mistaken." He should have come up with a better excuse. It sounded weak even to his ears, but he hadn't expected the woman to search Philippa out.

Philippa shook her head. "I am not. She said she is Mrs. Keates and handed me this." She pulled another letter from her reticule, then handed it to Weston.

Damn. This was similar in style to the information that Lord Germayne had forwarded to him. How much debt could one man amass? And why would Lord Germayne receive a demand for payment, only for Mrs. Keates to arrive and present Philippa with the same demand? Something didn't seem quite right. Extortion? Weston had interviewed this other Mrs. Keates on numerous occasions, and she did not seem the type capable of such tactics. Was someone coercing her into such actions?

"Let's start from the beginning." Reading the note again, he questioned, "What makes you believe that this woman is telling the truth?"

"I don't believe that she is telling the truth."

He glanced up and met Philippa's eyes. "If you did not believe it, you wouldn't be here."

She stood abruptly and began to pace. "Alright. I have my doubts. Not because of her, but because... None of this makes any sense. Why would he have lied to me?"

Weston could hear the restraint in her voice. He detested that she still had feelings for Keates. Before he could stop himself, the words spewed from his mouth. "That blackguard does not deserve your compassion."

"Don't call him that. He was not a criminal. He said..." She turned her back on him, her voice trailing away.

Strolling to the side table, she picked a small rose from the vase. "I have to know," she said as plucked the petals from the innocent flower. Her head whipped around. "Don't you understand? I have to know." Except for her flushed cheeks, her features were calm, emotionless, although her eyes told a different story.

Guilt was a powerful poison to swallow. Weston went to her. "I am sorry. I should not have said those words, regardless of my feelings."

She gazed at him with visible hurt and anger. He remembered that look. He had hurt her once before, but at that particular moment, he'd believed it was for her own good. If only he could turn back time.

"Why do you detest him?" It was an innocent enough question, but the answer was far too complicated and far from innocent.

He did not want to be the one to disillusion her with tales about her dead husband. He wanted to protect her. "I don't know what I am saying. Clearly, I didn't know him." That much was true. *Keep to the situation and the facts.* "What do you want me to do?"

She threw the mangled flower onto the table. "I want you to investigate this woman."

He *would* investigate her, *and* the letters, but he would *not* reveal the awful truth. He was certain that it would only bring Philippa more heartache, which was the last thing he wanted to do.

"Why not just let it go and begin to think about your future? You will be out of mourning in half a year. You are young and beautiful, and…" He stopped his sentence before he revealed too much of his own feelings.

Philippa's eyes met his. Those glorious blue eyes could melt any man's heart and have him begging on his hands and knees. He cleared his throat and mentally shook those thoughts from his head. Philippa was not and never would be his, but at the very least, he could protect her from the truth.

Instead of focusing on her elegant form, which had begun pacing the length of the room once more, he turned his attention to the letter that she'd received. He was looking for some clue. The whole situation just didn't make sense. Keeping his gaze on the note in his hand, he began to ask his standard list of questions.

"When did Mrs. …" Philippa eyed him with contempt. He was treading on unsteady ground. "…this woman visit you?"

"Yesterday afternoon, when Mother and Father were out." Philippa stopped in front of the fire, the light creating an aura around her. She turned to face him and scolded, "And before you ask, no, I did not tell my father. Since Aunt Imogene and I already had plans to travel to Hillhurst, I thought it best to bring the information directly to you."

This was going to be more difficult than Weston had imagined. "All right, so you did not tell your father. What did this woman look like?"

"She was shorter than me by a couple of inches and rather plump. Her clothes were not stylish, but presentable. Her hair was dark brown." She gazed past him as if trying to recall every minute detail. "She had hazel eyes and dimples."

Damn, it *was* the other Mrs. Keates. But they had an agreement. Why would she have ventured to London to see Philippa? He needed to proceed with caution.

After Keates' death, Weston and Lord Germayne had ensured that all unfavorable business was dealt with without Philippa's knowledge. Weston had even managed to keep the worst of it from Lord Germayne. He cared too much for Philippa to allow her, or her family, to endure the pain and gossip that would certainly follow if the *ton* learned the entire truth. The Germayne family had already endured enough scandal in recent years to last several lifetimes.

Weston could feel Philippa's eyes on him. She watched with interest as he reread the letter. How could he ease her conscience without revealing all that he knew? Perhaps he could protect her, help her discover some of the information she desired, *and* keep his secret.

Before he could weave a convincing half-truth, she spoke up in a quivering tone, her fingers worrying the handle of her reticule. "Please say you will help me. Ever since he died, and I learned he was a gambler, I have asked myself constantly how could I have not known? What else did he keep from me? Please, Weston, I *have* to know. I need to know." She turned away from him. The next words that she spoke were his undoing. "I feel like I am withering inside."

PHILIPPA STOOD SILENTLY for countless seconds. She did not think she had ever waited so long for someone to speak to her.

Please say you will help me, she chanted over and over in her head. *Please.*

Doubt crept up, settling heavily in her stomach. The last two years had taken its toll on her. She wanted to be free. She wanted to be herself. She had to know what kind of monster she had been married to.

The visit from the woman claiming to be Mrs. Alfred Keates had disturbed her far more than she was willing to admit. Ever since her husband's death six months ago, she'd experienced an array of emotions. It wasn't until she'd over-heard a conversation between her father and Weston two months after Alfred's passing that she had confronted them both and learned the truth of Alfred's nefarious activities. Although she suspected that much more was being hidden from her.

With each passing month, the feelings of sorrow and

longing that had consumed her in the beginning had given way to anger, hatred, and disappointment—all of which she'd kept to herself. Her only regret regarding the untimely death of her husband was that she had not been able to conceive, and her dream of motherhood would go unfulfilled.

Now, with this latest development, she had decided to handle the situation herself. She wanted answers, not to be brushed out of the room because she was a delicate female who needed protection. She loved her father dearly, but she was tired of being treated like a child.

She knew she could trust Weston. Through every wild escapade gone awry, every innocent action that turned to gossip, and every decision made without thought for consequence, there were two people in the world to whom she could turn to—Weston and her sister, Artemisia—although for this, she could not unburden herself to the latter.

She walked back to the brown leather chair and sat on the seat's edge, waiting, holding her breath in hopeful anticipation. She just wanted to know, and then perhaps she could move on and accept life as a childless widow.

Weston looked over at her, and for one brief moment, she thought he would refuse her. He exhaled a long, slow breath. "I will help you, but on my terms."

Clasping her hands together, Philippa said, "Thank you." The breath that she had been holding eased out. Her body relaxed. She did not know what his terms were, and she did not care. She would attain *all* her answers, as learning about Alfred's gambling was only part of what she wanted from Weston.

"I have another investigation that I must report on, and then I will look into this matter."

"Thank you…"

Weston put up a hand. "Before you go thanking me, you need to listen."

Philippa sat silently, her lips clamped shut. She folded her hands in her lap to keep them from trembling.

"I will not have you getting involved. I will see to this matter and then I will come to you."

Philippa nodded. She assumed this must be how he conducted his investigations, calm and collected and always in charge.

"Will you be staying at Hillhurst?"

"Yes."

"I am sure you have nothing to concern yourself over. Your father and I…"

Philippa grunted. "I wish everyone would realize that I can deal with more than they think. Everyone is constantly trying to… Never mind." She closed her eyes and sucked in a deep breath, then squeezed her hands tighter, trying to control the anger. "I will wait to hear from you."

Weston stared at her with suspicion. She shifted in her seat. *So, this is what it feels like to be interrogated.* Thoughts of running from the room back to the sanctity of Hillhurst flashed through her mind. She wished he would stop staring at her. It was most discomposing.

He pulled his gaze away, and hurried over to an elegant side table. Pulling the stopper from the bottle, he began to pour brandy. Was he as discomposed as she felt?

"Would you like one?"

Philippa shook her head. She needed to keep her wits about her.

Clearing his throat, he spoke over his shoulder. "I am curious about something you said earlier. When the woman introduced herself as Mrs. Keates, how did she address you?"

That was the part that had enraged her the most. This was why she had to discover the truth. She knew that if she could find the answers to her questions, then hopefully some semblance of a normal life could resume, although she had her doubts about that. She had created far too much gossip over the years, but she at least could hope for a quiet, peaceful life in the country, far from the *ton*'s wagging tongues.

"She thought…" She couldn't even say the word. Lowering her voice to a mere whisper, she began again, "She thought I was…"

Weston sat in a side chair across from her, then leaned in. "Was…?" He drew the word out, prompting her to continue.

"His mistress."

Weston was squinting at her. From the confused expression on his face, Philippa assumed he had not heard her. She was so upset by the thought that she'd been labeled a mistress she wanted to scream.

Weston leaned back in his chair. "I see." Clearly, he did not comprehend what she was saying.

"The woman thought that *I* was Alfred's mistress! Why are you not upset? I might be a little impulsive at times." That statement earned her a quizzical look. "All right, sometimes I can be more than a little impulsive, but I am a lady, and I would never dream of cuckolding a man, regardless of how unha…"

Weston's gaze snapped to hers.

Too much. Do not reveal too much.

The last thing she wanted to discuss was her marriage. Quickly changing the subject, she said the first thing that came to her mind. "How is Miss Albryght?"

"My sister is as stubborn as always." Weston ran his fingers through his brown hair, settling his hand behind his neck, and Philippa sensed that he could have said more on the subject. "Speaking of sisters, I was surprised to learn that you have not visited Artemisia."

"How do you know that I haven't been to Kettleworth?"

Had he been spying on her? She would not put it past her

father to hire their family friend to follow her. Since Alfred's passing, everyone had been watching her like a hawk. It was quite smothering. That was one reason she had decided to stay with Aunt Imogene, with only the occasional trip to London. At least with her aunt, she was somewhat free.

"Artemisia mentioned that you have not been to Kettleworth in recent months, that's all. I was curious as to why you hadn't?"

The unspoken question hung in the air between them. He watched for her response, but she would not give him, or anyone else, the satisfaction of knowing her fears or regrets.

She swallowed hard. "She is preoccupied with her infant." Not willing to elaborate further, she decided it was time to take her leave. She stood, clutching her reticule, and said, "Thank you for your assistance with the matter of that woman." She was finished with being interrogated. "I'd best be on my way."

∾

ABOUT THE AUTHOR

Bestselling, award-winning author, Alanna Lucas pens Regency-set historicals filled with romance, adventure, and of course, happily ever afters. When she is not daydreaming of her next travel destination, Alanna can be found researching, spending time with family, volunteering, or going for long walks. She makes her home in California with her husband, children, one sweet dog, and hundreds of books.

Just for the record, you can never have too many handbags or books. And travel is a must.

ALSO BY ALANNA LUCAS

Dancing Around the Truth

A Waltz with Destiny: Book Four

Mrs. Philippa Keates thought she'd found her happily ever after when she eloped, but two years later, she's named a widow. The horror of her husband's death, and then the shock of discovering that Alfred was a dissolute gambler, has forced Philippa into a life of seclusion. But when she is paid a visit by a woman claiming to be her late husband's wife and demanding recompense, Philippa knows she must emerge from mourning and discover the whole truth about Alfred. The one person who can assist her is her childhood friend, Benjamin Weston, for whom she once held a *tendre* until she realized he didn't feel the same.

Benjamin Weston, the illegitimate son of the late Baron Albryght, has made a name for himself conducting investigations for those willing to pay a high price for discretion. When Philippa arrives on his doorstep, begging for his assistance, Weston fears most of all that she will discover the truth. He insists that his investigations will be done on his terms, vowing to himself that he will continue to keep his distance from Philippa. But as he unravels her mystery, secrets of his own begin to come to light, and soon it becomes clear that there is more at stake than just Philippa's reputation.

Wish Upon a Waltz

A Waltz with Destiny: Book Five

Anastasia Quintin has resigned herself to live in quiet seclusion as companion to Miss Isabel Albryght, but one lost wager by her headstrong bookworm of a mistress soon requires Anastasia's return to the society from which she hides. Her first event in eight years is to be a house party in honor of the recently entitled Earl of Huntingdon, hosted by his haughty grandmother.

Dante, Earl of Huntingdon, is furious. His meddling grandmother, determined to find him a wife before the week is done, has thrown a party in his name. But his heart is not available. Since the death of his beloved Anna, he has shunned marriage, believing no other woman could replace her. However, his anger is quickly quenched when he waltzes with a fascinating young woman at the masked ball, but no sooner does the dance end than she rushes away, leaving only her mask behind her.

Anastasia, having been persuaded by Isabel to impersonate her at the ball, is in shock. She has just danced with Dante St. Clair, the very man who long ago stole her heart and thereafter dashed all her hopes and dreams.

Can one night, one waltz rekindle what was once thought lost forever?

Printed in Great Britain
by Amazon